—WINNER—

American Book Award

•

—NOTABLE BOOK OF THE YEAR—

The New York Times Book Review

•

—FINALIST—

The Los Angeles Times

Art Seidenbaum Award for First Fiction

"Graciela Limón's first novel, *In Search of Bernabé,* leaves the reader with that special hunger that can be created only by a newly discovered writer . . . At once **stark and resonant,** it follows the lives of half a dozen characters, most notably a suffering mother and her sons, two men who are moral opposites, caught up in El Salvador's bloody civil war . . . Her novel's grounding in the history of the period is clear and effective. In addition, Ms. Limón's prose is assured and engrossing. ***In Search of Bernabé* deserves a large audience."**

—Ilan Stavans, *The New York Times Book Review*

"In this **well-constructed** first novel about El Salvador during the civil strife of the 1980s. Limón tells a tragic family saga . . . **Compelling and chilling.**"

—*Publishers Weekly*

"**A tightly woven first novel** . . . Limón's keen eye for the ways in which ordinary individuals get caught up in extraordinary events rivals that of Joan Didion in her 1984 novel *Democracy.*"

—*Booklist*

*(Please turn the page for more extraordinary acclaim for novelist **Graciela Limón** . . .)*

Praise for Graciela Limón's
The Day of the Moon

"Graciela Limón's **commanding** novel follows four generations of the Betancourt family through five decades . . . Limón contextualizes her saga with crucially placed details of Mexican political and social history, providing a sharp critique of the Mexican class system while embedding **several passionate and eloquently rendered love stories**. Through multiple points of view, this novel **deftly explores one family's tragic reckoning** with issues of cultural identity, sexual autonomy, and interracial love."

—*Publishers Weekly*

"Limón is a gifted writer who deeply respects history, which is one of the reasons her work is so **appealing** . . . [*The Day of the Moon* is] cleverly told from the perspectives of several of the key characters, who narrate the same events from their points of view. It is a **delicious technique** that gradually reveals the entire story in all its complexity . . . The text is sprinkled with Spanish as well as Latin, which adds to the **authentic** depiction . . . This attention to detail provides much of the richness of this **fine** novel."

—*Multicultural Review*

"**A story rich in ideas and excitement, a suspenseful tale with memorable characters . . .** Murder, dismemberment, casting out, imprisonment, love, loyalty, and the lives of the spirits swirl through the pages of this novel and make it **hard to put down.**"

—Ellen Shull, *San Antonio Express-News*

Praise for Graciela Limón's
Song of the Hummingbird

"Graciela Limón's tale is **downright hypnotic** . . . There are some **extraordinary descriptions** of pre-Colombian culture . . . And always there's the pounding in the language . . . **Compelling.**"

—*Washington Post Book World*

"Limón's novel presents the account of Huitzitzilin, or 'Hummingbird,' a Mexica noblewoman present and outraged at the Spanish conquest of Tenochtitlán . . . **Highly readable . . . Limón tells a good story** and keeps alive, in a fictional setting, interest in this epic and doomed period of Latin American colonial history."

—*Choice*

Praise for Graciela Limón's
The Memories of Ana Calderón

"Abused by fate and family, Ana, the strong-willed protagonist of Limón's second novel, endures a life of extremes . . . **Frequently riveting.**"

—*Library Journal*

"Should awaken the conscience and compassion that drive and haunt every reader. Alive with the ruin of historical memory and a life of testimony . . . **A novel of absolute stylistic and social integrity . . . Honest and terrifyingly pertinent** . . . This is a story of the hard realities that command the contemporary choice between personal freedom and familial, cultural tradition."

—*Booklist*

Novels by
Graciela Limón

The Day of the Moon

En busca de Bernabé
(Spanish translation by Miguel Angel Aparicio)

In Search of Bernabé

The Memories of Ana Calderón

Song of the Hummingbird

Arte Público Press
Houston, Texas

This volume is made possible through the National Endowment for the Arts, a federal agency.

Recovering the past, creating the future

Arte Público Press
University of Houston
452 Cullen Performance Hall
Houston, Texas 77204-2004

Cover design by Mark Piñón
Original painting by Lynn Randolph
U.S. Peace Plan (oil on canvas), copyright © 1990
In the Permanent Collection of the Arizona State Museum.

Limón, Graciela.
In search of Bernabé / by Graciela Limón.
p. cm.
ISBN 978-1-55885-073-6
1. El Salvador—History—1979- —Fiction. I. Title.
PS3562.I464I5 1993
813'.54—dc20 93-12813
CIP

∞ The paper used in this publication meets the requirements of the American National Standard for Information Sciences—Permanence of Paper for Printed Library Materials, ANSI Z39.48-1984.

7 8 9 0 1 2 3 4 5 6 12 11 0 9 8 7 6 5 4

To my niece, Lupe Gómez, for her loving encouragement and patience.

To Michael Kennedy, S.J., for his limitless dedication to the people of El Salvador.

ACKNOWLEDGMENTS

I extend a special note of thanks to those friends and colleagues who generously read portions and, in some cases, the entire manuscript of this novel. I thank you for your ideas and guidance without which *In Search of Bernabé* would not have been possible.

I also thank those special *salvadoreños* who shared their individual hardships in leaving their country in search of a better life.

Finally, I sincerely acknowledge the efforts of Roberta Fernández, who edited the manuscript with insight and directness.

PROLOGUE

You have grown old in wickedness...the sins of your earlier days have overtaken you...beauty has seduced you, lust has led your heart astray. This is how you have been behaving with the daughters of Israel and they were too frightened to resist...

Book of Daniel, Chapter 13

I

Santiago de Nonualco - 1941.

It began when Don Lucio Delcano was nearing his seventieth birthday, and his only consolation had been to roam his lands in an attempt to escape boredom. On the day it first happened, the old man entered one of the sheds by chance and found a girl seated on a stool, milking a cow. Momentarily surprised by her, Don Lucio paused until his eyes adjusted to the shed's gloom. Then he looked carefully at the girl, and saw that she was beautiful. Her face was oval-shaped, and her eyes were large and luminous, ringed by long black lashes. He figured that she was thirteen, perhaps fourteen. Her small breasts were just beginning to bulge under the thin cotton garment she was wearing, and in his mind the old man pictured her deer-colored nipples. He felt a surge of shame because of his thoughts, even as he bent down to take a closer look at the child.

"¿Cómo te llamas?"

"Luz, Patrón."

When she whispered her name, he realized that the child was his granddaughter by way of a son he had fathered with an Indian servant. It had happened years before, but he had kept track of the woman and the boy. As he peered into the girl's dark eyes, Don Lucio remembered that his son had married a woman of African blood. The girl now staring at him was a result of that mating. He recalled also that at the time of the girl's birth his son had asked for permission to name her in Don Lucio's honor.

He felt captivated by the child. Desire gripped him. He shut his eyes, hoping his urge would go away, but instead he took her in his arms, and pressed her soft, mahogany-colored skin to his bloated body. Confused by his feeling for the child, the old man forced himself to walk away, unable to control the emotion that was taking hold of him. She was a child, his granddaughter even, but she had fascinated his exhausted imagination and awakened in him feelings he had not experienced in decades. He walked away struggling to forget her, but he thought of the girl all that night. The next day he headed for the shed hoping to find her there again.

He found the girl stooped over a pail of white, steaming fluid, and when she looked up into his eyes, she smiled timidly. Lucio glared at her for a long time, making her shift uncomfortably on the stool. The old man had not intended to do what he did next but he moved very close to her, opened the fly of his trousers, and without speaking, indicated that she should reach in, and touch him.

Luz visibly gulped while her eyes widened with fear. She knew that no one denied the master any of his wishes. She also knew he was her grandfather. Ever since she could remember, people had been telling her so. The girl fearfully lifted her arm, and reached into the black hole. Her hand was stiff and unmoving next to the old man's testicles, and he beckoned her to take hold of him. Luz shuddered involuntarily as she touched the limp flesh.

The old man's head wobbled backward on his thick neck, his mouth sagged open, and he sucked in a large gulp of air when he felt Luz's touch, but he felt his genitals slack and unresponsive. He then told her to caress him, but even though Luz followed his demands, Don Lucio's body remained inert, and he realized that he had indeed become old. He pulled away from the girl's hand and walked away filled with anguish.

Thereafter, the old man became obsessed with the child, and his daily habits changed. He knew he had fallen in love with the child, and he defended his emotions, denying the wrongfulness of what he was doing. He dreamed of Luz day and night, blocking out everything, even that she was his granddaughter. He dreamed of going away with her to a place where no one knew that he was rich and powerful. In his dream, he and the girl roamed the green fields skirting the volcanoes, coupling in a hidden cove, and Luz loved him above all things, promising to remain always by his side.

The day came when Don Lucio felt the potency of his dream surge through his body, and he knew that this time he would prove his love to Luz. He approached the girl in the cow shed, where he suddenly picked her up in his arms and carried her to a corner of the shed where he slid down to his knees. He pressed Luz against the wall, and with his eyes shut tightly against the gloom, he remained there for a long while.

His large hands trembled as he lifted her loose dress. Then he inserted his hands between her legs, inching his fingers slowly up her inner thigh and into her vagina. When Don Lucio felt they were both ready, he penetrated her, and Luz, paralyzed by fear, submitted to him. After the old man finished, he asked her if she would let him do the same thing to her when she became a woman. Without knowing why, she responded that yes, she would let him do whatever he wished, anytime he desired it.

Thereafter the girl was careful to hide her meetings with Don Lucio from the servants' prying eyes. Luz's secret, however, filled her with anguish. She thought that what she had provoked in her grandfather was shameful, and that it had been all her fault.

II

Don Lucio Delcano resembled an overstuffed mummy as he sat surrounded by his fawning, adulating brood. Delcano's skin had been milk-white in his early years, but decades of tropical and mountain sun had darkened it, so that his face now looked as bronzed as that of his native servants. His ponderous nose was supported by a long, drooping white moustache and his hair was no longer blonde as it had been in his youth, but white. His jowls were bloated, and no matter how much he tried to stick out his chin in an attempt to tighten his jaw, the rolling flab layered around his neck. Once tall and muscular, Don Lucio's shoulders now stooped. Whenever he shuffled from his chair, he dragged his feet wearily, and his arms hung over his distended belly.

"May God bless you, Father. You're still strong as an ox, and as handsome as a young man of twenty."

"Birthday greetings, Grandfather!"

"Joy and happiness! That's my wish for you this day, Padre."

The long line of Lucio Delcano's progeny filed past, congratulating him. Their faces smiled, but the old man knew that behind the masks was rancor and hatred. He knew his children and grandchildren wished death on him, and he realized he hated them with the same intensity that they felt toward him.

"Abuelo, you're looking splendid on your day. What a prince of a man you are. You must have the secret of the fountain of youth."

Don Lucio felt a repugnance for his family that matched his own self-loathing. As he glared at their faces he felt that each one, from the oldest of his sons to the youngest of his grandchildren, looked like animals.

"Excrement! Lies! Stinking flattery! A collection of miserable creatures. I've fathered the makings of a circus."

The old man muttered as his faded eyes scanned the large room, then rested on his oldest son Damián. Damián looked like a camel, he thought.

"A stupid one at that. Bubble eyes, draping upper lip, split at the middle, a fat nose. "

Don Lucio's gaze darted to the other side of the room and focused on a heavy-set woman.

"Hortensia. A mare, all flab."

Lucio stared at his daughter as she walked across the room, swinging her body from one side to the other.

"She would crack the plaster on the walls with that ass of hers if the room were any smaller."

Delcano shifted his body in the oversized chair. He looked to the side and saw his youngest son standing by Hortensia at the table.

"Anastasio. The sun fried his brain a long time ago. He's a tapir...hoofs...muzzle...".

Next to Anastasio, Don Lucio spotted Fulgencio..

"Ah! The snout of a weasel, the priest of the family...ha!"

Delcano knew why his son had chosen to be a priest. Fulgencio preferred the freedom that a skirt around his legs gave him. The old man grunted inwardly. He felt that his belly was on fire.

"Animals! All of them."

His eyes flitted from Ricarda, to Eliseo, to César. Their faces began to blur as Don Lucio suddenly realized that if they were brutish and dull it was he who was the distortion. He let out a loud snort, and the brood laughed along with him. He saw their purplish tongues, and his head swam with disgust. None of them had the intelligence nor the courage to earn a single *colón*. None deserved the lands and the silver that he had accumulated with years of hard work.

"¡Mierda! Shit, ordinary pigshit!"

Wearing the wide brimmed Panama hat that had become his personal emblem, Don Lucio lowered his face against his chest. No one could tell that he had escaped to the pleasures of his memories.

"Luz, you have been mine. Only mine. Why do you look at me with such frightened eyes?"

"Something to eat or drink, Lalo?" Don Lucio's wife's shrill voice brought him back to the moment.

He resented the name she had for him because she used it to impress others with her wifely devotion; yet, he knew that she had never loved him. The name cut into his nerves like a sharp knife, and he mumbled to himself, "I married a cow!"

Don Lucio looked into his wife's eyes. She was offering him a plateful of green lumps that someone had concocted in his honor. His stomach turning, he escaped his discomfort by returning to the girl.

"When I'm with you, I feel only my love for you. I hear nothing. I see nothing. You fill my soul. You make me forget who I am."

Don Lucio's memories shifted to an even more distant past.

He had been one of several brothers and sisters born in a small village near Santander on the northeastern coast of Spain. His father had been a sailor, a drunkard, who beat his children and their mother. Lucio had grown to adolescence dressed in rags, his belly always aching with the pains of hunger.

By the time he was fifteen, his father's abuse and the stench of rotting fish had become intolerable. From the taverns, voices spilled out into the streets with news about the opportunities that awaited a quick-witted man in America. And so one day Lucio went to the port where a merchant ship was being prepared for its ocean crossing.

"¡Amigos! ¡Vámonos a America! ¡Vámonos!"

Without knowing the vessel's destination, the boy jumped aboard and secured passage in exchange for work in the galley. The trip was long and difficult, and he suffered constant bouts of nausea. The meagerness of the rations doled out on the voyage emaciated him, and he walked off the ship in El Salvador at the Bay of Fonseca, his body bony and his face gaunt. He had also grown taller, and at sixteen, Lucio knew he had to act like a man.

He found in El Salvador a world filled with people of many colors, mostly impoverished peasants. He never again thought of his mother or of his brothers and sisters. Instead he gave himself to his new land, never questioning his actions or his motives, all the time knowing that someday he would be immensely wealthy.

"¿Abuelo, un café?"

The old man's baggy eyes looked at the eager face of one of his grandchildren. Irritably he waved the boy away, refusing to take food or drink from anyone. Once again, he recalled his youth. Slowly, he had amassed plantations, mines, cattle, and servants.

Don Lucio clamped shut his burning eyes, and in the darkness he saw the girl's body, the nipples of her small breasts. "They tell me that you'll soon be a woman. Come! Let me kiss your breast. Do not be frightened. Please!"

"Padre Manuel is here to wish you a happy birthday."

A servant informed Don Lucio that the priest from the city had arrived. The old man resented being interrupted by the presence of the priest. As he looked up at his family, Don Lucio noticed that they had stopped their chatting. All eyes were intently riveted upon him. Hortensia, Damián, and Josefina were inclining their ears toward him trying to snatch at least one word of the whispering. Shutting his eyes, Don Lucio sagged deeper into his chair, knowing that his silence would stir their curiosity even more.

Hunched on his throne, his eyes shut tightly, his elbows folded over his swollen belly, Don Lucio Delcano began to experience a new feeling. Dim, soft at first, it soon gathered momentum. In an instant Don Lucio realized that he was going to die and that he had not yet received forgiveness for the sins and offenses he had willfully committed.

"To be forgiven I have to repent. I have to feel sorry for what I've done."

Don Lucio's breath caught in his throat. His mouth gaped open. No, he realized he repented of nothing. He was even amused by the knowledge that he was going to die as if he were nothing more than an animal. He chuckled, then laughed loudly, and as his belly quivered and heaved, his family responded by laughing along with him. The harder Don Lucio laughed, the louder were their guffaws.

Suddenly, he began to feel loss of breath. He sensed that the collar of his shirt was tightening around his craggy neck. The buttons on his shirt and vest were constricting like snakes around his heart. Sharp fingers were squeezing his lungs. He was no longer laughing, and his eyes were filled with panic, as he attempted to cry out. But the merriment continued around him. The brood misunderstood, or pretended to misunderstand while their laughter intensified.

The noise began to recede from Don Lucio's consciousness. In its place he heard a distant tinkling of tiny bells, followed by the heightening sound of a rusty accordion and a squeaky violin. He recognized the tavern music from the town of his birth. Facing death, Lucio Delcano was once again a youth of fifteen, surrounded by toothless, long-nosed men with bald heads and dirty berets.

He blinked trying to focus on those faces of long ago. But he could no longer see. Air began to siphon out of his body as his eyelids clamped shut. He gasped and gurgled. His hands frantically fingered his chest as he began to lose consciousness.

PART ONE

Thousands thronged to the Basilica of the Sacred Heart...and joined a silent procession behind the cortege as it was taken to the Metropolitan Cathedral. The sealed gray casket of assassinated Archbishop Oscar Arnulfo Romero rested on the steps of San Salvador's huge Cathedral, a wreath of red roses at its head. Suddenly the outdoor funeral service was transformed into a tableau of horror: exploding hand bombs, wild gunfire, terrified crowds stampeding in panic. Before it was over, 35 people had been killed; 185 others had been hospitalized...others disappeared.

Time Magazine, April 14, 1980

I

San Salvador - March 1980.

Even though the size of the crowd was immense, a strange silence prevailed. Only the hushed shuffling of the mourners' feet and that of their intermittent prayers broke the stillness. The streets surrounding the Cathedral were clogged with people who had come from every sector of the city, and from beyond San Salvador. There were those who had left kitchens, factories and schoolrooms. Campesinos had walked distances from valleys and volcanos, from coffee plantations and cotton fields. They all came to accompany their Archbishop on his last pilgrimage through the city. Most of them wept, crouching close to one another, some in grief and others in fear. They pressed and pushed against one another hoping to see something, anything that might give them a sense of direction. They were nervous, knowing that every doorway could be a sniper's hiding place.

From the Basilica of the Sacred Heart, where the Archbishop had lain in state, the grievers filed toward the steps of the Cathedral's crypt. The murmur of whispered prayers and stifled sobs rose, crashing against the shell-pocked walls, swirling and tumbling in mid-air.

"Padre nuestro, que estás en el cielo, santificado sea tu nombre..."

Bernabé Delcano struggled with the crucifix he had been assigned to carry in the funeral procession. He was holding the cross high above his head, even though its weight made his forearms ache. His hands, which clutched the cross tightly, were stiff and white around the knuckles and fingertips. The young man, like his fellow seminarians, was dressed in a cassock which slowed down his movements. The intense heat made his head throb, and the public speakers that blared the prayers of the Mass only increased his discomfort.

He continually looked back into the crowd, making sure that his mother was not far from him. Bernabé felt assured each time he saw Luz's round face returning his glances, knowing that she, too, was keeping her eyes on him. Once, he held on to the crucifix with one hand and quickly waved at her with the other, but he didn't attempt that again, since the gesture almost made him drop the cross. Sweat formed on his neck and trickled down the inside of his shirt to his waist. He looked around him, seeing his mother's face again, but now the interference of faces and bodies made it impossible for him to get a sense of her feelings.

He looked at the faces of the other seminarians, hoping to catch a glimpse or a look that would indicate that their confusion was like his. Instead he saw blank, expressionless eyes. Only their lips moved in automatic response to the Our Fathers and Hail Marys mumbled by the priests at the head of the funeral procession. Bernabé looked beyond the faces of his classmates to those of the people. Some were lining the streets, but the majority walked behind the priests and the nuns, the seminarians and the altar boys. Looking at those faces, he was suddenly reminded of a painting. Once he had taken an art class in which his professor had dismissed the unit on cubism with one word: excrement. Yet, Bernabé had been fascinated by the pictures and examples shown in the textbook, and had spent hours in the library of the seminary reflecting on them. One of the selections had been entitled "Guernica," and the caption beneath the picture had identified it as the work of Pablo Picasso. Bernabé knew little regarding the artist, except that people argued as to whether he was a Spaniard or a Frenchman. What mattered to Bernabé, though, was the painting.

In it were fragments of human beings. The portrait showed incongruously shaped heads, rigid, outstretched arms, dilated eyes, twisted lips, jagged profiles, all scattered without apparent meaning. It also showed parts of an animal, the face of a horse. Bernabé had noticed that the animal bore the look of terrified human beings. Or was it, he had wondered, that the reverse was true, and that human faces looked like animals when they sensed their slaughter was near. The odd thing, he had thought at the time, was that those broken pieces of human beings could not be brought together again, even though he had attempted to imagine a head attached to some arms as he tried to piece together a human figure.

Now, as Bernabé marched in the cortege, he realized that these people around him were really fragmented: faces, eyes, cheeks, and arms. They were broken pieces just like in Picasso's disjointed painting.

"Ave María, llena eres de gracia..."

The cortege wound through the streets, past the indifferent eyes of the wealthy, and past those who pretended to be wealthy. Their tight lips betrayed a feeling of disgust. It was a pity, those faces said to Bernabé, that the Archbishop had not heeded his finer instincts, his better judgement. Their eyes betrayed their beliefs that priests had best stay out of politics and confine themselves to Mass and to forgiving.

"Gloria al Padre, y al Hijo, y al Espíritu Santo..."

Bernabé began to feel fatigued; faces blurred in front of him. The endless prayers droned monotonously in his ears. The cross seemed heavier with each minute. As he moved along with the rest of the mourners he began to stumble on the wet pavement. His fingers went numb and his perspiration made the cross slip in his clutching fists. Suddenly, he dropped the cross and fell on his knees. His cassock got entangled around his ankles and the press of people from behind kept him down, forcing him to crawl on his hands and knees.

Bernabé jerked his head right and left. Unexpectedly, a loud blast shook the ground under his hands. A grenade exploded in the midst of the surging crowd at the edge of Plaza Barrios facing the Cathedral. The blast was followed by machine gun fire and rifle shots that came from several directions making the mass of people panic. Hastily, the Archbishop's body was picked up and taken into the church by four bishops. Most of the mourners, however, were unable to reach the sanctuary of the Cathedral, and could not find shelter anywhere. They swerved and lunged in every direction, screaming hysterically.

Mothers crouched wherever they could in an attempt to protect their babies. Men and women pressed against the Cathedral walls hoping to find cover behind a corner or a sharp angle. Young men, mostly guerrillas, pulled out hand guns, then fired indiscriminately into the crowd in an attempt to hit members of the death squads with their random bullets. Uniformed soldiers suddenly appeared, also firing automatic weapons into the crowd.

The plaza was soon littered with bodies of the dead and the dying. People pushed and trampled each other in a frenzy to survive. No one thought. No one reasoned. Everyone acted out of instinct, pieces and fragments of tormented beasts driven by a compelling desire to live. All the time, the blasting and the firing of weapons and grenades continued.

Bernabé, crawling on the asphalt, was caught unaware by the first blast. The shifting weight of bodies pressing above and around him made it impossible for him to rise. Then bodies began crashing in on him, pinning him down. Suddenly, he felt intolerable pain as someone stepped on his hand, grinding the bones of his fingers against the pavement. He screamed as he attempted to defend himself with his other hand, but it was to no avail. The boot swiveled in the other direction, stepping on Bernabé's hand with an even greater force. The crowd dragged him back and forth, finally smashing him against a wall. Managing to pick himself up with his left hand, he leaned against the stone wall and looked at the bobbing heads and twisted limbs. The panic was at its peak.

"¡Mama-á-á-á-á!"

Bernabé's scream was hoarse and choked; it emanated from his guts, not from his throat. He didn't know what to do, where to go. His wailing rose above the howling of those around him, and he continued screaming for his mother.

The pain in Bernabé's arm was intense, forcing him to remain against the wall despite his urge to run. He remained motionless, feet planted on the bloodied concrete. His body was bathed in sweat and his face, neck and hair were caked with dirt, grime and blood. Bernabé began to sob, crying inconsolably even though he was a man of twenty years. He screamed because he feared he was going to die, and he didn't feel shame, nor did he care what anyone might think.

Suddenly the thought that his mother was also in danger cut short his panic. Bernabé lunged into the crowd, kicking and thrashing against the bodies that pushed him in different directions. He screamed out his mother's name, using his able arm to raise himself on whatever shoulder or object he could find, trying to get a glimpse of her. But his mother was nowhere in sight.

Bernabé was able to get away from the plaza, slipping through a break in the encircling cordon of soldiers. He ran around the fringes of the square several times. He rushed up and down streets, and into doorways, shouting her name, but his voice was drowned out by the din of sirens, the horrified screams of people, and the blasts of machine guns. Bernabé shouted out his mother's name until his voice grew hoarse and his throat began to make wheezing, gasping sounds.

He suddenly thought that she might have gotten out of the plaza and run home. So he scrambled toward his house, hoping that he would find her waiting for him, but when he arrived there the door was locked. With his good hand, he beat on the door. When his fingers became numb with pain, he banged with his forehead until he felt blood dripping down his cheeks.

Suddenly a brutal shove sent Bernabé sprawling on the pavement. When he looked up he saw an armed soldier standing over him. "What are you doing here, Faggot? Better pick up your skirt and find a church to hide along with the other women. If you don't get your ass out of here, your brains are going to be shit splattered all over these walls. You have until the count of five. Uno, dos, tres..."

Bernabé sprang to his feet and ran. He kept running even though his breath began to give out, even though the pain in his arm was intolerable, even though he knew his mother needed him. Panic gripped at his guts and his brain. He knew he had to keep on running.

After the horror had spent itself in the plaza, stunned men and women searched in the lingering blue haze for a son, or a wife, or even an entire family. Among them was Luz Delcano. She called out her son's name, her soft weeping joining that of others, like the rotting moss that clung to the stone walls of the buildings surrounding the square. Luz Delcano went from one body to the next, taking the face of this one in her hands, turning over the body of another one. Desperation began to overcome her. In her fears she remembered the loss of her first son Lucio. Now Bernabé, her second born, was also gone.

Government troops had taken control of the area. They ordered all stragglers to go home, and not to return. Luz Delcano had no choice but to follow the orders.

II

The day was ending, and Bernabé was too fatigued to continue running. His lungs felt as if they were about to rupture, and he was forced to stop abruptly, gasping through his open mouth. The plaza was behind him, but he didn't know what to do next, so he followed three men who were leaving the city, heading in a northern direction toward the Volcán de Guazapa. As he followed, Bernabé tripped over his torn cassock several times, each time hurting his broken hand. He tried to tear off the long garment, but it was impossible for him to undo the front buttons with only one hand.

As they moved closer to the volcano, Bernabé realized that there were others besides him heading up the same path. Without asking, he knew that they were going up into the mountains, to the guerrillas' stronghold. He saw the crowd growing. People appeared from everywhere, trickling into the group from behind trees, from under shaded awnings, from the entrances of houses and huts. There were people of all shapes and ages. Men walked side by side with grandmothers. Children and adolescents as well as old men mingled with the crowd. Young women, many of them pregnant, others with babies and older children at their side, walked, taking short, rapid steps.

Bernabé saw that they were mostly field workers, men and women with hardened hands and leathery faces. As he looked around him, he saw people whose eyes were small from squinting in the harsh sunlight. Their lips had tightened against pain and humiliation, against suffering. Most of them were dressed in tattered clothing. The women covered their heads with faded shawls, and the men wore ragged trousers and threadbare shirts, their heads covered with frayed sombreros, yellowed and stained by years of sweat. Their feet, some clad in rough sandals, others bare and toughened, pounded the volcanic earth which rose in dusty gusts. The evening air was tinted with hues of yellow and gold, and the shadows of those men and women lengthened in the setting sun.

Bernabé was bewildered by what was happening to him. He looked at the unknown faces swirling around him, trying to understand the events of that day. He was afraid, but not knowing what to do, he continued walking as if in a daze, caught in the press of bodies that pushed him forward.

The crowd continued its trek up the skirt of the volcano, but came to a sudden stop when another group, armed men and women, appeared from behind a ridge in the mountain. They rushed forward embracing as many of the newcomers as possible. Bernabé suddenly found himself surrounded by a cluster of smiling, laughing, jubilant men, women and children. He felt as if he had stumbled onto a carnival or a fiesta; there was handshaking, hugging, and back-slapping. He turned in circles, looking in every direction, thinking that perhaps he was the only stranger among them, when unexpectedly two arms encircled him from behind. Bernabé turned and looked into a face that seemed friendly. He returned the warmth of the embrace.

"Me llamo Nestor Solís."

"Yo soy Bernabé Delcano."

Nestor Solís was more or less Bernabé's age. He was dressed in faded pants, and a coarse white shirt that was half-buttoned, exposing his bronzed chest. He wore heavy boots. A straw sombrero shaded his eyes. Like his compañeros, he was armed with a weapon which he wore strapped across his chest. As he spoke, Nestor's eyes were bright with exhilaration at the wave of new recruits joining the ranks of the guerrillas. When he smiled, Bernabé saw that several of Nestor's front teeth were missing.

"Are you a priest?" Nestor asked.

"No, not yet, and I suppose I never will be now."

Bernabé heard his words and he was shocked by what he had uttered. The thought of not returning had not crossed his mind. When he spoke again, his words were hesitant.

"I, well, I think God has other plans for me. I suppose. Someone else will have to be a priest in my place. Maybe I'll have to stay with you." As he said these words, Bernabé lifted his arm in a broad curve to include the guerrilla force. Even though he had used his able arm, the motion had caused him to flinch.

"You're hurt. Is it bad?"

"No, Señor. It'll soon pass."

Bernabé lied, for his hand was hurting more than ever. He momentarily forgot his pain, though, when an armed, powerfully built man called for the attention of the crowd.

"¡Bienvenidos, compañeros y compañeras! Soy el Capitán Gato. I'm here to welcome all of you, and to let you know that you're safe. Up there, beyond that mountain, you'll find shelter and protection. You might want to return to where you came from but, on the other hand, you might want to join us. You'll have time to find out for yourselves."

He paused, as if expecting someone to ask a question, but there was silence, interrupted only by the sound of wind sliding off the volcano's side. Capitán Gato had more to say to the crowd.

"We're still a long way from the end of our road. We must march past Presa Embalse, then up the mountains of Chalatenango to where our other brothers and sisters are waiting for us. It's going to be difficult, so you need to help one another."

After a brief rest, the exodus of men, women, and children resumed the journey. Nestor kept close to Bernabé as they moved forward. He pointed out the trails used by the guerrillas and explained what he knew of life in the mountains.

"Listen, compañero, don't assume that I know everything just because I can show you a thing or two. In fact, I haven't been up here for too long. I'm really a campesino. I was born on a small piece of land where I lived all my life with my mother, my father and my two sisters. The two girls are younger than I am."

Bernabé was listening to Nestor with interest. He glanced at him as they walked. When Nestor stopped talking, Bernabé questioned him. "Why did you join the guerrillas if you're a campesino?"

Nestor licked his lips as he concentrated on his answer. "Not so long ago, just last January, one evening when we were eating our dinner, four soldiers broke into our house. It happened so suddenly that none of us could do anything. My father's ankle had been broken in an accident he had with the mule, so he couldn't even stand up. When I tried to defend my mother and my sisters, I got smashed in the mouth with a rifle butt."

Nestor was again quiet; he seemed to be brooding. Bernabé decided not to ask any more questions, but his companion suddenly began to speak again.

"They wanted something to drink, so my mother gave them water. Then they said they were hungry, so we shared what we were eating."

When Nestor paused, Bernabé looked at him and saw that the vein in his neck had swollen, and that he was swallowing rapidly. Not knowing what to say, Bernabé kept quiet.

"Then one of the pigs began to laugh, and he said that he was hungry, but not for the maize we were eating. He was looking at my sisters, and I knew what he was saying. I'll tell you, compañero, I hope you never feel what I felt at that moment. I was afraid, but at the same time I felt rage pulling at my hair."

"I jumped at the pig, and grabbed his filthy throat. Then everything went black. One of them hit me on the head with a rifle. But the blackness lasted just a few minutes, because when I opened my eyes I saw that my father had crawled to one of the *mierdas* and had taken hold of his ankle. The animal shot my father in the head. When my mother tried to reach my father, the soldier shoved her so hard that she fell to the floor."

"Por favor, compañero, don't tell me any more. Let's just keep quiet while we're walking."

"No, no, I need to tell you what hapened. *¡Esos marranos!* It was easy for them. While one aimed his gun at me and my mother, the others did what they wanted with my sisters. They forced them to take their clothes off in front of us. They were laughing and making filthy noises with their teeth. The girls fought. They kicked and scratched, but that only excited the shit eaters more. They took turns making my sisters kneel down in front of them. They forced them to suck their pinga, all the time yelling '¡Más! ¡más!'"

"Then they took the next step. They raped them. When the filthy pigs were tired, like animals, they went over to the table and ate what was there. Then they left."

Nestor began to choke, but he regained his voice in a few moments. "Sometimes I feel bad because I left my mother and sisters to come here, but I couldn't think of any other way to make those animals pay for what they did to us. Here I have the opportunity to look for the pigs. Each time the compañeros capture a handful, I am the first one who looks at them. You think it's impossible for me to find those soldiers, don't you? Well, compañero, I'll tell you, you're wrong. I remember that one of them had a scar that crossed his face from his ear to his nose. I'll recognize that one's face even at midnight! Sooner or later he'll show up."

In the two days it took the group to arrive at the guerrilla headquarters in the Chalatenango mountains, Nestor and Bernabé continued talking. Travel had been slow because of the number of the group and the scarcity of food, but when they arrived they were happy in spite of their fatigue and hunger. As they walked through the center of a small, makeshift village, Bernabé was surprised by the dwellings he saw. Houses, sheds and shelters had been carved out of the lush mountain forest, and even though the shacks were tiny, they were sturdy, and they provided shelter and safety.

Bernabé now felt less pain in his hand. Still wearing his torn, mud-caked cassock, he walked with the rest of the group as they were noisily welcomed by the guerrillas who had been expecting them. Men and women waved their hands, calling out, "¡Bienvenidos, bienvenidos!" There were women outside of each hut, their cooking gear in place. Bernabé, who was famished, saw griddles placed over inviting fires with *pupusas* and other appetizing foods piled on them. He noticed with even more interest that the women were armed, and that each woman had a weapon which was leaning carefully against a rusty tub, or a tree stump, or some other place nearby. He also saw that each woman, regardless of age was wearing a bandolier stuffed with ammunition.

Bernabé thought of his mother, and he tried to imagine her dressed like those women. To his surprise he found it easy to picture her among the other women.

"You would be right there, Madre, welcoming me and the other new people. Your legs would be spread apart, planted in the dirt. You'd be wearing one of those big sombreros, and you'd like the ammunition belt that everyone wears here. Your arms would be folded over your chest as if to let everyone know that you were capable of being a dangerous person. Sí, mamá. You would be a good guerrilla!"

He caught himself smiling at his thoughts. But when he looked around, he felt confusion and fear gripping him. When night approached, Bernabé was shown where he was to sleep. There, a young man pointed to the cot that would be for his use. He told Bernabé that he would be leaving soon but that in the meantime he would be happy to help him. Bernabé welcomed the man's friendliness, and asked him his name.

"Arturo Escutia," was the brief response.

The following morning, when Bernabé awoke, he noticed that the young man was gone. He wondered why Arturo Escutia had not asked him for his own name, then did not give the young man another thought.

III

"No one here has ever asked me my name, Madre. When I marched into the compound wearing my long coat, everyone thought that I was a priest, and ever since, I've been known as Cura. Well, I could do nothing else but accept my new name, just like the rest of the compañeros, especially the jefes, who are called Gato, Cirilo, Pájaro, Chato, and other names that sound like these. La Pintada, la Nena, la Doctora; that's how the women are called.

"It was good I let them call me by another name because it proved to the compañeros that I was one of them. I know in my heart the guerrillas have made me one of their own, even though I didn't spend my life with campesinos like them.

"Still I feel like an outsider. No one knows that I blundered into them because I was confused and scared. All I ever wanted was to become a priest."

Bernabé spoke to his mother as if she were standing next to him. He worried about her constantly, and his fears were complicated by the knowledge that he had crossed a forbidden line when he followed the crowds up the mountain. There were spies, even among the ranks of the guerrillas, he knew. *Orejas* they were called.

"If I return to the city, and to you, the spies will find me. Like dogs, they smell everything. They'll arrest me and kill me, maybe even kill you. All I ever wanted was to help people, to minister to them. Now I'm afaid I'll be forced to kill people. Madre, I'm ashamed of my fears."

To all appearances, Bernabé had become part of the guerrilla band. No one knew that each day he felt great anxiety. At night his fears took control of him, robbing him of sleep and within a few weeks those sleepless nights began to take a toll on him. He thinned down to skin and wiry muscles, and his face hardened and aged beyond his years.

Unaccustomed to the rigor of mountain living, Bernabé hated the crude ways in which the compañeros lived. His stomach turned with the stench of the makeshift outhouses, and he was plagued by the clouds of mosquitoes that bit him day and night. He was embarrassed at having to bathe naked in front of the women of the band, and was ashamed to admit he was profoundly disturbed at the sight of men and women openly engaging in sexual acts.

He knew that he was different, and he wrestled with this, knowing that it isolated him from the rest of his companions. He tried to become like them, hardened men and women, accustomed to the bitterness of pain and death. "I am not them. And you made me this way, Madre. I don't know what it is to be pushed away from my land, to see my sisters attacked like Nestor's, or to see babies burned and killed. Around here, they all talk of *el Escuadrón,* of being tortured by government agents. I had never even been in a demonstration. All I ever saw was what happened the day the Archbishop was buried."

For days and weeks in the mountains, Bernabé learned how to become a guerrilla. He felt pride mixed with apprehension when he was issued a weapon and cartridge belt. Without betraying his ignorance, Bernabé draped the sling diagonally across his chest while he held the rifle stiffly because the wound in his hand still ached. He stood rigidly at attention, his feet together and knees locked; then he arched his back, and held his head as far back as he could just as he had seen soldiers do when they stood on the street corners and plazas of San Salvador.

The discipline of guerrilla training was difficult for him, especially in the beginning. The new recruits, male and female, were awakened at four in the morning when they were given a few minutes to dress and splash water on their faces before joining the group for a breakfast of tortillas and coffee. The day's training followed immediately.

The new members were splintered into groups of eight or ten men and women each headed by a veteran instructor who taught them the basics. These exercises were intensive, causing the newcomers severe fatigue and pain, and in his weariness at the end of each day, Bernabé thought of abandoning the group to take his risks in the city, even to face the possibility of torture or death. Each morning, however, he renewed his decision to remain as part of the force.

The training program for the newcomers included hours of marching. At times their feet blistered and bled. The new guerrillas learned the tactics of hand-to-hand killing, and also how to shoot from behind rocks, or how to hang from the limb of a tree. They were instructed on how to be prepared to wait in the darkness to catch the enemy off guard, to learn to make a weapon from whatever was at hand since a firearm would not always be available. They learned to convert a tin can into a jagged, cutting instrument and to transform an ordinary stick into a gouging and throttling device. They were trained for quick, solitary movements. And they were prepared especially to die alone.

Bernabé and the other beginners had trained for a month, when their leaders decided it was time for them to move out of the stronghold, and head north towards the Sumpul, the river seperating El Salvador and Honduras. The order was given for twenty-seven of them to prepare for a march the following day at dawn.

Bernabé was unable to sleep that night. When Chato came to his hut to awake him, Bernabé was already out of his cot, putting on his trousers. He dressed himself in the clothing he had been given when he had first arrived at the camp: old denim pants, a faded cotton shirt, heavy boots, and a panama hat. His jacket had belonged to a government soldier, and when Bernabé had first gotten it, the garment still had the patches of a corporal as well as the soldier's name. At the time, Bernabé removed the emblems because he was afraid they would bring him bad luck. The faded spots had remained, however.

"*¿Listo?*"

Chato's voice was muted, but clear.

"Sí. I'm ready."

At Gato's signal, the group marched north. The first few hours of the trek were quiet and uneventful. All they heard was the crunch of branches and leaves beneath their boots. Soon one of their scouts returned to report that a large group of civilians was at the river, apparently intending to cross into Honduras. Without hesitating, Gato ordered his band to make its way to those people whom they might be able to assist in the crossing.

When they neared the river, the guerrillas stood on a ridge that gave them a wide view of the action. Bernabé was astounded by what he saw. Four or five thousand men, women and children of all ages, were milling around. Many of the adults were old. Some hobbled on canes, or makeshift crutches, or clung to someone else. Babies were carried in a mother's or brother's arms; many young people appeared to be alone. Dozens of women were pregnant, and the men, even he apparently able-bodied ones, looked lost, dejected, and weighed down by an invisible burden.

Bernabé was shocked to see so many people. From his vantage point, he could see that many of them were already at the edge of the river attempting to cross over to the other side. He turned to the others of his group hoping to see what could be done. There were no boats or canoes, or even rafts, with which to cross the river's deep spots and its tricky currents. Anyone could see that if the refugees were to reach the other side, they had to ford the river either by swimming or by finding its shallow spots.

Bernabé's head began to throb with panic. He clamped shut his eyes, hoping that the sight would evaporate, that when he opened his eyes the mirage would have vanished. But when he looked again, the people were still there, buzzing like mosquitoes, melting into an immense blob of blacks, blues, and browns. He was afraid and confused, and he cursed himself for having been caught in that trap.

Suddenly, army helicopters appeared, casting long shadows over the crowd as they swooped lower and lower. People began to scream and to shift wildly from side to side as they sought cover from the guns overhead which suddenly, indiscriminately, began to fire on targets. The revolving blades of the helicopters sucked the air, tearing at the refugees' hair and clothes as the loud whirring deafened the people's ears to their own fearful screams. When the attack began, Gato ordered his followers to retreat, but most of them panicked. In his confusion, Bernabé separated from the main group, thrashing about in the bushes, making abrupt false starts. He zigzagged in different directions, reversing his steps, losing his balance. He bumped against trees and crashed into bushes. Then he lost his rifle and hat, and his hands and face began to bleed from the scratches and cuts. Once, he fell in a small hollow in the ground, and as his fingers dug into the moist volcanic earth, pain flashed from his wounded hand up his arm, and he screamed. Finally he was able to free his feet from the mud that held him down, and he ran, not away from the helicopters and the terrified people, but mistakenly straight into them.

Most of the fugitives had been able to run for cover behind rocks and thickets, but some were caught off-guard and without the possibility of escape. Those who were at mid-river when the attack began were the first to be gunned down. As they were hit, their bodies somersaulted into the air like mannequins or rag dolls, plunging head first into the swirling waters of the Sumpul. Others were riddled by the helicopters that buzzed overhead and by the machine gun fire of soldiers that had by now come out of the underbrush, firing at will.

It was into this cluster that Bernabé had blundered. When he realized what he had done he tried to go back, but the shoving and pushing bodies made escape impossible. He was knocked to the ground, and although he attempted to stand several times he was forced down each time. He stopped resisting, and instead arched himself into a ball, while bodies crashed down on him. Automatically he clamped his muddied hands over his eyes. At one point he looked through his fingers long enough to see a boy held in his mother's arms ripped apart by a piece of shrapnel. It happened so quickly that even the woman did not realize what had happened.

Bodies and pieces of limbs piled on top of Bernabé. Certain that he would be buried alive if he didn't move, he sprang to his feet, screaming. "¡Mamá! ¡Ayúdame!"

Crying for his mother's help, Bernabé plunged head-long toward the river. His unexpected thrust caught the soldiers off guard, stunning them for the few seconds he needed to escape. Confused by his sudden appearance, they stared at him, mouth open, instead of firing. Bernabé ran with his arms rigidly stretched forward, as if sleepwalking, and his hair, plastered with blood and excrement from bowels that had been torn-apart, stuck out in a grizzled aura. He screeched as he ran, and his howling sounded inhuman, like the baying of an animal.

As he streaked toward the river, his strange appearance triggered the refugees into moving, for they felt that he knew the way, that he was commanding them to run, to follow him across the river to Honduras, and to safety. Like him, they also screeched in defiance, lurching after him. Men, women and children pitched forward, oblivious of the helicopters that hovered above them like giant flying scorpions. As they pressed ahead they trampled past the soldiers, who were still confounded by the sight of the howling specter that had arisen from among the dead. Everyone ran forward, their arms stretched out rigidly as they yelled and strained to reach the other side of the river. They continued following Bernabé because they saw that his feet found the shallowest, safest route across the river. Where he stepped, the reddish waters of the Sumpul receded, exposing flat stones on which they could run.

Panting, driven by terror, his chest splitting with pain, Bernabé kept running even though he had already reached the other side of the river. He didn't know in what direction he was headed, but he didn't care. His body was in command, ordering him to go on.

The troops, unable to cross the river into Honduras, stood gawking, machine guns hanging limply from their hands. They turned to their commanding officer for his orders, but he only gestured obscenely towards the other side of the river. The helicopters dangled in the gloomy air, unable to cross into foreign air space.

No one knew for how long or how far into Honduras the people had stampeded before their pace lessened. Bernabé, his body nearly doubled over, staggered and stumbled as he took each step, dragging his feet, swerving clumsily as if he had been drunk. His arms hung limply by his sides, while his head wobbled grotesquely. Nearly an hour passed before he realized that behind him followed hundreds of people. This was the last thing he remembered because, no matter how much he tried to focus on what he was looking at, objects and colors began to blur, until there was only blackness.

When he awoke, Bernabé was in a gloomy hut with two women tending to him. They worked in silence. One was rubbing his arms and chest with a wet cloth, and the other was preparing food over a fire set on the earthen floor.

"Señoras..."

His voice was shrill and seemed to tremble. The women nodded in recognition, but remained silent. Bernabé leaned back onto the mat trying to reconstruct what had happened to him, but he could only remember that he had blacked out after crossing the river.

"Señoras, is everyone safe?"

"Sí, hijo. Most of them. Thanks to God, and to you."

"Where are we? Have I been here a long time?"

"We're in Mesa Grande, but you have been in the other world for three days. You've been calling your mother. Many times you whispered, '¿Mamá, mamá, dónde estás?' You could not hear her answer, and so you cried out that you were afraid. You can see that she did answer your calls. She has returned you here to us."

IV

More than any other Delcano, Lucio was distinguished by milk-white skin, blue eyes, and hair shaded so fairly that it often appeared golden. It was because of his looks that others spoke of him as the Angel. He was thirty-eight years old, tall, lean and muscular. He had a long nose, a broad forehead that people said signaled intelligence, and the straight, tight lips that betrayed his family's well known arrogance. Like many of the other Delcanos, Lucio was a success. He was a colonel, as well as a highly positioned officer in Army Intelligence.

Those few people who thought they knew him well, believed that military life was his sole interest in life. Unknown to anyone, however, the colonel's public side was dwarfed by an intense brooding. When he was in those moods, secret thoughts were more real to him than anything else. No one imagined that his musings and monologues preoccupied him more than his achievements or the power he had amassed over the years.

He was seated at his desk. On it were official documents and a red telephone. Its line led directly to the presidential offices, and it rarely slipped Colonel Delcano's mind that only a few people possessed that privilage. He had been staring out the plate-glass window, absorbed in thought, when he silently swiveled his chair to glance at the documents neatly placed on his desk. One of those papers was a source of annoyance because it communicated that yesterday, at the Sumpul River, a section of his battalion had surprised several hundred campesinos who were headed towards Honduras. His soldiers and several helicopters had stumbled onto the subversives by accident, and what now irritated Colonel Delcano was that the soldiers' attempts to halt the maneuver had not been successful. The soldiers had managed to deter some two hundred of them, but the rest, estimated at between seven and twelve hundred people, had been able to cross the river.

The colonel's set jaw betrayed his irritation. He had an impeccable reputation, but even a small incident such as the one described by the communiqué disturbed him. His battalion had the best equipment, the best trained soldiers, the best intelligence information. He would not allow subversives to laugh in their face. Colonel Delcano made a mental note to look further into the details of the incident. Someone would have to pay a price for the mishap.

His eyes again turned to the window, trailing off beyond the rooftops of the compound. Putting the Sumpul incident aside, he turned to images of his past life. As he often did, he tried to recall some small detail of the day his mother had sold him. He had been only a few days old when she had handed him over to the Delcanos. His aunt Hortensia had verified this story many times over, fixating it in his mind, where it haunted him relentlessly, filling him with doubts.

"Hortensia said my mother was a worthless opportunist from Spain who presumed that she could worm herself into our family by having a Delcano child. When she was told that under no circumstances could she ever marry a Delcano, she soon changed her tune. The old man would never permit such a marriage."

"I did not believe Hortensia's story. Too many questions were left unanswered. Why did my mother abandon me? Was it really only for money? Or was it for something she sensed I was? She must have thought I was shit. Otherwise she would have fought off tigers to keep me with her. No. I never could believe Hortensia's story. Surely, there was another reason why things turned out as they did."

Lucio's life had been lonely in spite of the fact that the family had seen to it that he received whatever he needed. He had attended the best schools in San Salvador, and when he turned eighteen, he had enrolled in the American military academy, where he not only learned to plan and execute battles, but to perfect his English as well.

He was the sole Delcano heir because despite the old man's many children and grandchildren, the family had been plagued by catastrophes, and Lucio wound up as the only survivor in the family. The boy with most promise, Anastasio's middle child, choked to death on a chicken bone when he was fifteen. Of Ricarda's three sons, each turned out to be an idiot, incapable of caring for himself. Domitila's children had all run away and no one knew of their whereabouts. Damián had married a wiry, nervous woman who seemed to be a victim of *mal de ojo,* for all her pregnancies had ended either in miscarriage or stillborn children. Finally, there was Hortensia, obese and given to alcohol. She had never married. Instead she had seen to Lucio's upbringing.

The family had known who the child's father was, so he was given the name Lucio. However, Damián and Hortensia forced a pact on the brothers and sisters, who agreed never to disclose to the child that he was really their brother. Instead, he would always pass as one of the grandchildren.

Lucio Delcano had always felt empty when he was a child in spite of the material things he had been given. When he was old enough to ride, he had gotten his own horse and, later, when he became a young man, he had been treated to a flashy, expensive car. But he had never experienced the one thing he craved: a mother's love and attention.

"Hortensia always acted as if she were my mother. But she just played the role so others would think that she was good and that she had sacrificed herself for me, for she wanted to hide what she was actually doing to me.

"When did it all start? When I was still a baby? The first time I can remember the incident was when I was about four years old. I was in bed, and she had her hand inside my pants, rubbing, and squeezing me. Strange noises were coming out of her throat.

"Hortensia did these things to me until I was fourteen. Then, one night when she called me to her bed I discovered that this time she wanted more. I felt sickened and, even though I was confused, I didn't do what she wanted because for the first time in my life I wasn't afraid of her. Nothing would make me put myself into her body. So I started to move away. That's when she took hold of me, pressing and squeezing my penis until I knew that if I didn't get away, I would faint or die from the pain. I grabbed her neck. My fingers sank into its fatness. I pressed as hard as I could. Her eyes bulged. Her skin turned purple, and her tongue jerked in and out of her mouth.

"Hortensia was strong. She was able to throw me off the bed and smash the lamp on my head. I felt everything turning black when I fell on the floor, but when I saw that she was going to hit me again, I grabbed the chamber pot that was under her bed. She never expected her own shit to come flying in her face!"

The phone on the colonel's desk buzzed, startling him. He glanced down at his hands. They were rigidly flattened on the desk top, and his fingertips were a whitish blue from the pressure.

"Dígame."

"Coronel Delcano, we've been notified that many of the subversives that were attempting to reach Honduras yesterday have returned. They have now been able to make their way back to the capital. Some as far as La Libertad."

"Why are they returning?"

"Señor, unfortunately some of them escaped our men. But since they were unable to make it across the border they are returning. They are coming in this direction. It seems that although many were wounded, they still have been able to move. Our reports indicate that most of the traitors have been sheltered by foreign troublemakers and religious fanatics, as well as by other types of civilians. Gringos, most of them. The bad part of the situation is that the traitors who tried to cross the Sumpul are telling everyone that they were ambushed, and slaughtered like cattle by government soldiers."

Lucio Delcano was now faced with the problem of witnesses. He hated untidy work, and he was especially displeased by complications. "What were our men doing? How can we explain unarmed campesinos escaping our soldiers?"

His voice was sharp, penetrated with frustration and sarcasm. He listened for a response. The answer at the other end of the line was faint and hesitant. "I'm sorry, *Coronel.*"

"I want the names of the officers in charge of yesterday's skirmish. I also want the names of the foreigners involved. I don't care what or who they are. Nuns, workers, whores, whatever and whoever they are. I want their names, and I want that information now!"

Colonel Delcano returned the phone to its cradle. The word *whore* had again evoked Hortensia's image and also that of his uncle Damián Delcano, who had never left the family home, even after he had married. Damián made sure, however, to keep silent on most matters, and he deferred to his sister at all times and on all issues regarding money, the household, the workers and, especially, the upbringing of Lucio.

"I always felt sorry for Damián, especially because he was afraid of Hortensia. He was unlucky, too. Unlucky mostly because he didn't look like his brothers and sisters. Because of this, people laughed at him. They mocked him because he was bald and fat, and because he shuffled like an old monkey. But he was kind, and he tried to help others, even those who jeered at and misunderstood him.

"I liked him. Maybe I even loved him. He tried to be a father to me. Most of the time we never even spoke, but I knew that it was fine, because somehow he knew what was inside of me. At night, it was he who put me to bed. Every night he kissed my forehead, and said, 'Buenas noches, hijo,' And when I wasn't in school, he let me be at his side as he did his things. I did that because I liked being with him. But we both knew there was another reason why I wanted to be with him.

"'Tío, which one of your brothers was my father?'

"'The third oldest. He died very young.'

"'What was his name?'

"'The same as yours.'

"'But, I thought that I was named after my grandfather.'

"'My brother, too, was named Lucio, and since he was named for our father, you can say that you also are named for your grandfather.'

"'But...'

"'Hush, Lucio! You're giving me a headache. You're named after your father and your grandfather. Accept it, and that's enough for today.'

"'But Tío if my father was the third oldest, and if he died young, how could he have had me? You've always told me that I'm the youngest of all the Delcanos. And, what about my mother? Is Hortensia saying the truth? Did my mother really sell me to you?'

"Damián never answered that question. But still, I loved him, especially when I saw that his sister hated him. She liked to make Damián feel bad in front of his wife, and the servants, especially when she got drunk. She called him names of animals, and she said things about what he and his wife did in bed. But my uncle was always silent. He had no words for Hortensia. I used to wish he'd defend himself, and I prayed that one day he would hit her. But he never did, and I knew why. He thought that he was filth. Just like me.

"I remember the night Hortensia decided to get even with me right after I threw shit in her face. We had finished eating, and she was drunk. Damián's wife left the room. I think that she had sensed what was to come. But my uncle stayed. And I stayed with him. Then Hortensia began. The words she vomited that night changed my life. She twisted my soul, making me hate myself and anyone who ever touched me. Damián implored her to be silent but she was determined to let it all out.

"'You're not my nephew,' she yelled at me. 'You're my brother!'

"Hortensia opened her mouth letting out her hatred against me.

" 'You're the brat of a filthy mother who sprang from a litter of African slaves, animals who grovel in dirt, fornicating and spawning without knowing who or what they are! You, might look like an angel, but on the inside, you're nothing but a black devil! Don't fool yourself!' "

" 'You despicable worm, it's time you realized that your mother was just like you! A pervert! Yes! Yes! Yes! You're hearing my words as you should have heard them a long time ago! Your mother fornicated with her own grandfather!'

" 'And remember this, you piece of burro shit! Remember that you were born in a filthy hut, with no more than raw dirt for a floor. That's here your mother dropped you from her belly. On dirty, filthy dirt! So don't boast about yourself! Don't believe for one second that trash about being an angel!'

" 'Why did the family take you from the bitch that was your mother? Because we couldn't tolerate her bragging that she had given birth to a Delcano. That's why! It was easy. All we had to do was jingle a few *colones* under her nose, and there it was, we never saw her again! Ha! Money! It's magic!'

" 'And where is your mother now? Well, I'll do you the favor of telling you that she's common servant in one of the homes in Escalón. There it is, the truth for you to lick, and to swallow. You're free to go to that rich neighborhood anytime you wish. You're free to guess which one of the army of brown sluts who work there is your mother."

"Hortensia asked me what I was. Was I her brother or her nephew? She laughed when she asked me what I was to myself, because she said that I'm both my own brother, and great-grandson at the same time, and that I'm twisted. Deformed. A monster that might as well have my ass where my head is!

" '*¡Monstruo!*' "

"Hortensia screeched the word, pounding her fist on the table, and the thumping noise bounced off the walls shattering my insides. I couldn't move, I was anchored to my chair. But her words captivated me, even though they thrashed my heart and my guts, even though her obscene hatred was ripping apart my heart. And I believed it all. I believed it, not because I wanted to, but because at last, I was finally hearing the truth! I accepted it all because what Hortensia screamed no longer held contradictions for me, as Damián's foolish, clumsy explanations did. I believed her because at last I knew why I had always felt that I was nothing. I was a Delcano, but I was deformed, warped.

"When I looked at Damián I saw that he was trembling, his hands shook as if he were a very old man. And I? I could only stare at Hortensia. I couldn't cry, and I couldn't say anything, but when her mouth began to quiver and her cheeks twitched, I knew then for the first time that something in me frightened her. So I glared at her until she lowered her eyes. After that she shut them tight.

"Suddenly, I wasn't nailed to the chair anymore. I got up, and walked out into the darkness, and over to my room where I stayed with my eyes open until everything got black and I lost consciousness. And then, for the first time, I had the nightmare. In my dream I am always a twisted, ugly creature. My limbs are in pieces, and the parts are in the wrong place. My legs are where my arms should be. They grow out of my shoulders, and my arms are down there, where my feet should be, and in place of my head are my testicles. I am indeed a monster.

"Next day I found out that Damián and his wife had gone away. I never saw them again, and I was left alone to hate Hortensia all by myself. I used to spend hours looking at the portrait of the old grandfather, the one that had hung in the main room ever since I could remember. I had never noticed that picture, but now I sat and stared at it until my eyes hurt. Now I knew that he was not my grandfather. He was my father! I looked at him, at his big belly, at his flabby chin, and I told myself that that was how he looked when he and my mother created my life.

"After that, whenever Hortensia called for me, she used one word '*Monstruo*'. But I never spoke to her again. Never!

"One night Hortensia was in the middle of one of her fits. I could hear her in the kitchen, banging into chairs, smashing plates and glasses as she cursed and mumbled. Suddenly there was a loud thud, followed by a bouncing sound, like a sack of flour tumbling off a shelf. Then everything was quiet. It scared the servants because they knew that something had happened. And they were right. One of them came to my room to tell me that Hortensia had fallen down the cellar stairs. I ran as fast as I could wishing with all my heart that she would be hurt. When I got there I saw her sprawled at the bottom of the stairs and I realized that she couldn't move her legs. She looked up at me. 'Get me out of here!' she whispered.

"That was the last time Hortensia ever spoke to me, but I didn't hear what she was saying because I was listening to something else. I closed the door, locking it, and putting the key in my pocket where no one could reach it. Then I called the servants into the kitchen. 'Go to your rooms, and don't return until I order you.' Her screams lasted three days becoming more and more faint until finally there was silence."

"Does your head hurt, Colonel Delcano?"

Lucio had not heard his clerk rap at the door, then let himself into the office. "No, no."

"Señor, I'm trying to gather the information you've requested but..."

"Information? What information?"

"Why, the names of the officers in charge of yesterday's incident, and the names of the agitators helping the subversives who tried to cross the Sumpul. I've been able to get some of the names you need. Here's the list. I regret that it's incomplete, but tomorrow I'll do my best too."

"Sí, sí. Well, get it to me as soon as possible."

"It's late in the day, *mi Coronel.* Should I stay on to..."

Delcano bluntly interrupted the clerk. "You want to go, don't you? Why don't you come out and say it? Get out! I'll expect you here no later than eight in the morning, and I want complete details and information before noon."

The man disappeared behind the door. The sky was growing dark, and it would soon be night, but Delcano did not light the lamp on his desk, preferring instead to remain in the gloom. Finally, when darkness forced him to switch on the light, he glanced at the document the clerk had placed on his desk. Neatly typed on white paper was the name of one of his officers identified as having been in charge of the skirmish. Next to that name, in a tidy column under the title "Activistas," Colonel Delcano read the names of several foreigners.

A brief report followed. The activists were identified as agitators and spies to whom the survivors of the Río Sumpul incident were flocking for shelter, food and assistance. In the colonel's estimation the worst part of the report was the statement that people were now referring to the incident as the May First Massacre.

Colonel Delcano drummed his fingers on the polished surface of the desk. Witnesses were the one thing he would not tolerate. Now the officer's sloppiness had created a potentially serious problem. But, he, Colonel Delcano, would handle the consequences. He flipped the report face down, and tucked it under the blotter.

V

"These people.... Who are they?" Colonel Delcano's voice was calculating as he interrogated his clerk.

"Mi coronel, we know that they're mainly foreigners and fanatics. I think that some have been here a long time..."

"You think! You think!" The colonel's voice was a hoarse whisper. It was strained, and his words betrayed irritation. "I want you to do more than think. I want you to bring me accurate, precise information. In the meantime, call in the lieutenant in charge of the Sumpul maneuver. I want him here in my office before evening. That will be all. You may leave."

The clerk left the room silently. Few people had the courage to return Colonel Lucio Delcano's glassy stare, much less attempt an exchange of words with him. His demand for exact information was nothing new. He was a feared intelligence officer, known for the strict manner in which he conducted investigations. Since his early childhood when he had pressed his uncle Damián for details about the family he had gotten into the habit of gathering information. His talent for ferreting out material, for prying and digging had been perfected during his youth when he had become secretive, cagey, and greedy for what others might have to tell him.

Lucio had been fourteen when he left the Delcano estate, but even then he had been filled with rancor and hatred. When he entered the military academy, he was prepared beyond anyone's expectations to deal with a new way of life. He had plunged into his career with vengeance and spite and his primary tools had been spying and the amassing of information to be used against his enemies.

Cadet Delcano became known among his fellow students and teachers for his intelligence, self-control, and seemingly limitless ability to know and remember details. He soon knew the birthplace of his companions, their birth dates and the names of every member of their families. He remembered their choice in sweets and colors as well as their favorite movies. What his companions didn't realize, however, was that by knowing everything important to them, Lucio was gaining control over them.

His teachers quickly noticed Delcano's ability to manipulate circumstances and people, and it was not long before they tapped him for their own benefit. When he became a spy against his classmates, he embarked upon a profession that would eventually take him to the top levels of government.

After completing the requirements of the academy, Lucio had been sent to the United States where he learned quickly. He became skilled in the language of the Americans and in their ways, mastering their preoccupation with order and organization. Especially appealing to him was their method of gathering, sorting, and cataloguing useful information for later review.

When Lucio returned from the United States he had been placed in the intelligence gathering sector of the military, where he applied his fine-tuned skills. From the beginning, he demanded that even the most insignificant detail be considered important and pertinent. Every bit of data was to be rigorously divided and sub-divided, sifted, measured and maintained under strict alphabetical and numerical order.

He became invaluable in the military structure, and his star rose not only because he was a son of the privileged caste, but because he was talented and cold-blooded, and his ability to work seemed limitless. From his early days in military intelligence, and especially after achieving the rank of colonel, Lucio almost always remained in his office late into the night, long after his staff had retired for the day. It was during those hours that he would read and analyze information submitted by his agents. His stamina and ability to work provoked awe in others. No one knew, however, that sleeping was an intolerable agony for Lucio, and that he feared falling asleep because then the nightmare would assault him. No one imagined the shrewd colonel felt a child's terror of the dark nor that it was chronic insomnia that led to his efficiency.

Colonel Delcano's office was at the core of intelligence activity. It was directly to him that heads of death squads reported, as did others charged with the business of assassination. As a result, politicians and other fellow military officers, as well as judges and lawyers were afraid of the angel-faced colonel and of the power he exerted. Everyone knew that the invitations to high society dinners, weddings and baptisms, which always included Colonel Delcano, were extended out of fear of his powerful position.

Outsiders were not the only ones to be targeted by Lucio's probing. He applied the efficiency of his profession to his personal life as well. He remembered the first lead that Hortensia had given him in what soon became an obsessive tracking down of his mother: "She is a common servant in one of the homes in Escalón."

From the time that Lucio had first left the family residence to study at the academy, he had utilized every moment of his free time attempting to find his mother. He had little to go by, almost nothing in fact, since the wealthy section of the city held dozens of households, each with its own staff of servants. He had to find one woman out of hundreds, perhaps even thousands who fit the same description. The search took Lucio several years, but he eventually did uncover Luz's whereabouts, based on a dim description of his mother provided by Damián. She had been a girl, thirteen or fourteen at most, when she bore him, Damián had said. Thus, he figured that his mother would then be around twenty-eight years old. Also, he knew that her name was Luz. Of that not only had Damián spoken, but Hortensia as well. He remembered hearing that his mother had very brown skin and large eyes. She was short and rather plump.

Even though the description might fit countless women, Lucio continued his search. He spent hours, and eventually months and years, seated at bus stops where he scrutinized women. Finally, he concluded that he was looking in the wrong place. More than likely, his mother lived in the mansion where she worked. Therefore, she would have no need to take buses, or any other form of transportation. Rather, she would shop at the market or in other stores that sold household goods.

Lucio shifted his attention and began to haunt marketplaces. He stalked the streets daily, walking up and down Avenidas 8 and 10, and through the Mercado Cuarte, a maze of stalls where servants went to purchase the day's food or garments for their masters. Lucio frequented the other marketplace as well, the one located on Calle Gerardo Barrios behind the National Palace. This market was always filled with servant girls, idlers, peddlers, and stray dogs.

He spent his time looking at women's faces, hoping to see something of himself in one of them. He soon became conspicuous, not only because of his white face and fine clothes, but because of his strange manner of staring. People began to talk about the intruder who went from one stall to the other, from one store to the next, asking if anyone knew a woman by the name of Luz. The time came when people anticipated Lucio's question, answering before he had the opportunity to open his mouth.

"No. ¡No conozco a ninguna mujer que se llame Luz!"

One day his persistence paid off when he approached the driver of an elegant car. The chauffeur was standing by the automobile, his arms crossed over his chest as he waited for his passengers.

"Señor, forgive me, but do you happen to know a woman by the name of Luz?"

When Lucio asked his standard question, the man seemed surprised. He took a few moments before responding. "Luz Delcano?"

Lucio's breath left him. He felt the blood in the veins in his head throbbing. Delcano! He had never stopped to ask himself what her surname might have been. He cursed his stupidity. His face drained, and the man asked him if he felt sick.

"Do you want to sit a moment inside the car? Let me bring you a glass of water."

"No, no, gracias. It must be the heat, nothing else, believe me. Tell me more about this woman, señor. Where is she now? Where can I find her? What does she look like? What..."

"¡Un minuto, por favor!"

The man held up a hand, as if to shield himself from a hail of invisible stones. "One question at a time, please! To begin with, who are you? And what do you want with Luz Delcano?"

"Perdón, I'm Lucio Hidalgo and I have a gift of money that my grandmother left for the lady who, I understand, was a servant of my family when she was very young."

As Lucio fabricated his lies, he placed a large amount of money in the driver's hand, who smiled with obvious satisfaction. "¡Gracias! But I'm afraid you're a little late. You see, Luz left about a year ago."

Lucio could not bear the possibility that, after he had dedicated four years of his life to his search, his mother would be slipping through his fingers. He pressed the man for more information.

"Tell me where I can find her. You see, I promised my grandmother just before she died that I would find her former servant. I cannot fail in my promise. Please tell me where Luz Delcano has gone. Or, if you don't know, tell me where I can get more information about her whereabouts."

"Well, I'll tell you only because you look like an honest boy. You see, Luz stuck her foot in it. You know what I mean? She stepped on the plant that causes women to puff up like this." The man used his arms and hands to indicate a big belly. "It turned out that the seed was planted by Señor Grijalva, the master of the house. So when la Señora found out, well, you know... ."

The man's voice trailed off, but his eyes were bright with mockery. "When Luz left the house, she hadn't had her kid yet, but I heard around town that she had a boy. Must have been some months back."

Lucio felt his feet sinking into the ground. For a few seconds he had the impression that the sky was lowering itself, coming closer and closer to him until it would suffocate him. A son! His mother had another son. He had a brother. Someone eighteen years younger than he.

"Where can I find her? I must know!"

"Well, if you must. She went north, to a little town called Carasucia. You might know where it is. It's on the border with Guatemala."

Lucio turned his back on the man without thanking him, or looking back at him. His tears felt hot on his face and he could taste the salty drops as they ran down his cheeks and chin, scorching their way down his neck, staining his white shirt. He had found his mother, but now she had another son. He wept as he realized that he had searched for his mother not because he hated her, as he had told himself from the beginning, but because he loved her, and he could not deny that he had secretly hoped that she, too, would love him.

Despite his desire to confront his mother, Lucio did not have the courage to go to her new home. Instead he went through a period of depression. He stopped eating, becoming gaunt and withdrawing into himself more than ever. He was forced to admit that he did not have the strength to face his mother, and that he feared her ridicule. He knew, however, that he had to keep track of her.

The plan he worked out then was only the beginning of a method that he would perfect throughout many years. He hired people to spy on Luz and her baby. Through those informants, Lucio built up dossiers on both his mother and his brother in a process that spanned years. He continued this practice even when he was in the United States, where he received envelopes stuffed with papers and photos of the boy and Luz.

Even though Lucio never doubted his actions, he was often

assaulted by the many questions left unanswered. He wondered if his mother would sell his brother as she had sold him. He had no answer to that question nor to the one that had always nagged him: whether or not his mother had actually sold him for money. Trying to ferret out the answer, he sent his agents back to the family estate to question the few servants who still remembered Luz Delcano. All of them acted nervously, however, and provided little of the information he sought.

Those years of probing were painful for Lucio because as soon as one of his agents would deliver a written report, he would bury himself in it, reading and re-reading all its details. Through these communications he learned of his mother's life, of how she cooked and sold food, and of how she cleaned the homes of the few rich families in Carasucia. It hurt him to find out that despite her menial work, his mother had a happy disposition, and that others loved her. When people described her as affectionate, he felt cheated.

His spies informed him about everything that had to do with his brother, from the child's first steps, to his early days in school. He knew that his brother was intelligent, that he grasped his lessons rapidly, and that he tended to help other boys and girls. Lucio was especially tormented when he read that the teachers and the parents of the other children loved his brother.

A source of even greater torture was the constant supply of photographs he received. In time, these photos became an obsession, and Lucio spent nights compulsively staring at frayed, faded snapshots of his mother cuddling the child or of her pointing at an unseen object while the baby laughed. Most of those pictures became so familiar to him that soon he did not even need to look at them to recall them as vividly as if they were in front of his eyes.

Through the network, Lucio knew every move his mother and brother made: her decision to return to San Salvador, the manner in which she supported herself and the boy once they were back in the city, and, eventually, his brother's adolescent decision to enter the seminary.

When Luz and Bernabé had first returned to the capital, Lucio had even felt compelled to go to her, to confront her with the way she had abandoned him. But fearing that she would reject him once again, he never approached her.

Recently, the colonel had been informed that on the day of the Archbishop's death, his brother had fled to the mountains, and there joined the guerrillas who now called him *Cura*. Colonel Delcano also knew that his mother had been seen roaming the barrios of the city, pounding on doors and windows, asking for her son.

"*Mi Coronel*, I'm afraid it's getting late. Shall I call in the lieutenant?"

"Sí. And don't interrupt us until we're finished."

Almost immediately the lieutenant walked in and stood rigidly at attention.

"*Mi Coronel*, at your orders!"

"Be seated, *Teniente*. Please make yourself comfortable."

As he spoke, Lucio Delcano's voice was flat, cold, filled with icicles. "I'll get to the point! I'm disappointed with the way events turned out at the Sumpul the other day. I understand you were in charge."

"*Sí, mi Coronel.* I can't explain what happened. We were able to plug some of the subversives, but others got away. My men... something strange happened. The campesinos began to run. They followed a madman who ran out to the river. Our choppers, well, if there's blame, it belongs to..."

Colonel Delcano stiffly lifted his hand, palm outstretched in the lieutenant's direction. "Enough! You're not here to give me excuses. You'll have to try to show a better face next time."

Delcano was on the verge of reprimanding the lieutenant for his carelessness. He even considered demoting him but before taking this measure, he paused. The man was too valuable as an expert in terminating enemies. Clearly he was a better assassin than a soldier and it would be best not to hold him liable for what happened at the Río Sumpul. The colonel took a different approach.

His voice changed. He seemed to be giving a warning. "In fact, *Teniente*, since you've been instrumental in resolving incidents of continued agitation among the people, I feel you should be given the opportunity to redeem yourself regarding the Sumpul fiasco."

The lieutenant smiled, relieved at the change of attitude he perceived in his superior. The colonel then extracted a sheet of paper from under the desk blotter. The lieutenant knew it was the report on the agitators assisting the Sumpul escapees. By carefully placing the paper on his desk, then running his fingers over it with care, Delcano conveyed the importance of its contents to the lieutenant. Then, he leaned back in his chair and reclined his elbows on the armrests. Slowly, he placed the fingertips of both hands together, forming a triangle under his chin.

"*Teniente*, we have many subversives among us. There are several of them, foreigners, intruders, troublemakers, who have been distorting the news of events in our country. Most recently, and I know this will interest you, they've been spreading lies regarding the Río Sumpul incident. This report," Colonel Delcano delicately held the page between his index finger and thumb, "although as yet incomplete, explains their activities. These people claim to be assisting needy campesinos but, in fact, what they're doing is circulating Marxist rubbish. It's embarrassing for us all. We must think of the bad example they give others, mustn't we? People will begin to believe in what these lies preach. Who knows, others may even attempt to imitate them. Therefore, they must be silenced...permanently."

Colonel Delcano paused, allowing his words to take root. "At any rate, I know that I needn't be detailed about what I mean." He focused his pale gaze squarely on the lieutenant's face.

"I understand, *mi Coronel.*"

Colonel Delcano's voice then became smooth, soft, like the voice of a father advising a young son on how to remove a nail from his bicycle tire, or how to repair his favorite plaything. There was no expression on his face.

"You'll know how to take care of this embarrassing matter, I know. I feel confident that there's no need for me to provide suggestions. What I do have to say is that this office is at your disposition insofar as information and any other necessary assistance are concerned. As for timing, again I leave that up to you. I set no deadline for the task. Take your time, please. It might be a matter of days, but then, you might need months. Who's to know? All I request, and this you already know from working for me, is that precision and efficiency be your guides. No more sloppiness, please!"

The lieutenant's jaw and neck jerked slightly. "All of them, *mi Coronel?*" he managed to ask.

Colonel Delcano stared at the soldier. He nodded his head, then whispered his orders through frozen lips. "*Sí, Teniente.* Todos. Every single one."

PART TWO

Her son was waiting for her...

The Child That Never Was
María Virginia Estenssoro

I

After the massacre, Luz Delcano scoured the streets of San Salvador for two months looking for her son Bernabé, but every lead given by acquaintances and even strangers turned up empty. In her search, she found that the city was under a pall of terror and confusion because a new wave of killings was hitting the streets. Some foreigners and even some of Luz's acquaintances were disappearing. Bodies, mutilated beyond recognition, were being discovered daily.

Many of Luz's friends, leaving everything behind, were flocking to bus stations with no other aim than to escape El Salvador. The majority of them were heading up to Mexico, and some as far as the United States. Young men were leaving jobs and families because rumors spread from street to street telling of youths being kidnapped at gunpoint by patrols, then being forced into the army.

These events, as well as her futile search for her son, bewildered and frightened Luz. She felt dragged and torn by forces beyond her control, for she could not believe that Bernabé might be dead, or even that he had been pressed into the army. Yet, she didn't have a clue as to his whereabouts. Those around her began to convince her that her son must have fled the city along with the other young men, and that more than likely he had headed north. But where to the north? Her friends shrugged their shoulders and rolled their eyes when Luz asked this question.

As weeks slipped by and Bernabé's whereabouts remained unknown, Luz's intense desire to find her son finally overshadowed her apprehensions. Putting aside her emotions she decided to join the others in their northbound trek, blindly hoping that her son had done the same thing. Uncertain of where her road would ultimately end, she purchased a bus ticket for Mexico City knowing that she would not be alone since others were following the same course. Luz figured that once she got to that city, she would determine her next step.

On the morning of her departure, Luz woke up early. She gathered a few things and packed them into a cardboard box taking only the indispensable: a change of clothing, something to sleep in, a shawl, a small purse with the *colones* she had salvaged after selling some of her things, and a blurred snapshot of Bernabé in his seminarian's cassock.

While she waited on the damp pavement outside the crowded station, Luz began to experience a new barrage of emotions. She felt foolish and stupid for what she was doing. But as she hesitantly put her foot on the running board of the bus, she suddenly sensed the grief of those around her, and she realized that besides searching for her son, she was fleeing just as they were. She was struck by the thought that if she was leaping into the dark, so were they; and they were doing it because they had no other choice.

"Por favor, señora, súbase o hágase a un lado."

"Perdón. Sí, sí."

Inside, the second-class bus smelled of rancid fruit and bodies. As she craned her neck, she caught a glimpse of the other campesinos also leaving El Salvador. Mostly, they were sullen men with toughened hands and eyes that were tiny slits. All of them wore battered, ragged and sweat-soaked straw hats. There were also women aboard the bus. Some were young, clinging to children, and others were old. Most of them wore faded, stained aprons. Luz again drew comfort from the look on their faces, for she realized she was not the only one who was afraid.

She moved to a seat next to a window and with a sigh she placed her tattered possessions under her. Luz was fifty two years old, and her weight made moving difficult. As she sat down she got a glimpse of her reflection on the grimy window. Her hair was matted and messy, her cheeks were puffy and her chin was flabby. For a moment she stared at her image, knowing that if people could see inside of her they would see something worse. The image of Don Lucio Delcano flashed through her mind. Guilt gripped her heart. He was standing in front of her, in the cow shed, and he was taking hold of her hand. She shut her eyes tightly attempting to erase the recurring memory of her youth.

Then unannounced the bus driver cranked on the motor. At first it had seemed unable to turn over. Then with a blast from the exhaust pipe, the engine coughed, sputtered and took hold. The passengers jerked forward as the driver stepped heavily on the throttle. Luz turned to bid farewell to her country. The last image she saw through the rear window of the bus was the dome of the Cathedral.

The driver promptly asserted his authority by using a severe tone with his passengers. He ordered each to remain in his or her place, to keep their possessions close by—he would tolerate no thievery—and to keep the kids from running up and down the aisle.

"¡Llegaremos a Guatemala en cinco horas!"

In the beginning, the trip seemed smooth, even though the creaking and roar of the engine blocked out the passengers' voices and conversations. The flat highway, however, soon became bumpy and filled with holes. Each time the bus rocked, heads wobbled back and forth. By the hour, the sun's rays beat down on the thin metal roof of the bus, intensifying the heat inside.

Five hours later, when the bus crossed the border into Guatemala the passengers were relieved, thinking that they would be allowed to spend some time outside in the fresh air, but the man in charge of immigration merely waved his arm signaling the driver to go ahead. Later on, when they arrived in the capital city, the bus headed directly to the station where it collected a few parcels and packages bound for Mexico City. Finally, the passengers were allowed to get out of the bus for half an hour, and all of them rushed to the rest rooms to empty out their bladders.

The trip through Guatemala was uneventful and hot, with only occasional stops as before. Late on the evening of the second day, the bus made its way across the border separating Guatemala from Mexico. Luz felt the bus slowing down, so she sat up and wiped a small section of her window in an attempt to find out where they were. She read a sign: Talismán, México.

"¡Todo mundo, abajo!"

This time it was a Mexican immigration agent who was shouting orders. Everyone had to get out of the vehicle for inspection. Luz got up from her seat with difficulty because her feet had swollen terribly and her shoes were painfully tight. Some of the passengers were mumbling and complaining. Others asked what was happening and why they weren't continuing on to Mexico City.

When the bus finally emptied out, the passengers were lined up against its side. The night was dark and the only light came from a fly-speckled yellow bulb that hung by a wire over the entrance of a squat bungalow. There was a sign above its door: Inmigración. Los Estados Unidos de México.

Two men in uniform reviewed the passengers' documents one by one. It was so dark that Luz wondered how they could make out what was on those papers. Suddenly she saw that a young male passenger was being separated from the group. One of the Mexicans pushed the man, then shook him by the shoulders.

"What have we here? A deserter! That's what you are, aren't you? What is your name, cabrón? ¡Rápido! Answer when you're asked a question!"

"Arturo...Arturo Escutia," the young Salvadoran responded, visibly shaken. He looked confused and terrorized.

"Bueno, mi Arturito. Anyone can see that you're a coward."

As the man spoke, other uniformed individuals appeared out of the darkness. They jeered and goaded the young man, taunting him with accusations.

"What are you anyway? A communist?"

"Sí. You have the shit-loving face of all communists!"

They roared with wide open mouths, while the Salvadoran passengers looked on, some paralyzed with fear, others in frustrated anger. Suddenly, the first official pulled out his revolver, and held it to the young man's head. "¡Pendejo! Don't you know when you're in danger? Are you going to stand there and say nothing just like a god damn, stinking burro?"

It was clear that he was expecting something from his victim. Escutia was obviously supposed to respond or to offer something. But he was speechless with fear. Luz saw the barrel of the revolver gleaming in the dark, and when she realized that it was pointed at the young man's head she could not restrain herself. In her mind, Arturo could have been Bernabé. Both young men were about the same age and height, and they both had the same look in their eyes. An excruciating heat rose from Luz's belly up to her neck. Something like hot vomit filled her mouth forcing her to open it wide. A terrifying wail escaped from her throat.

"¡No! ¡No!" she shouted over and over. "¡No tiene derecho!"

Moving with unexpected swiftness, Luz lunged at the arm of the man holding the weapon, and began to struggle with him. Man and woman toppled to the ground, tangled in a wrestling bout that stunned the on-lookers. For a moment, everyone was shocked, but soon they were struck with the humor of what they were seeing. They began to laugh out loud, including Arturo. A circle formed around the two wrestlers. Several people rushed up, craning their necks and stretching their backs in order to get a glimpse of what was happening–an unheard of match between a woman and a man.

Rooting and applauding broke out.

"¡Una mujer y un hombre están luchando! ¡Qué barbaridad!"

"¡Dále en la chingada!"

"¡Eso! ¡Chíngalo bien!"

They all cheered for Luz, even the Mexicans in uniform. With her hair sticking out wildly, she pounced her short, fat body on top of the skinny agent, knocking the wind out of his belly. He grunted, and even though he tried to push the woman off, all he could do was kick and jiggle his legs in the air. Luz straddled the man with her knees and, with her hands grown strong with the wringing of wet sheets, she took hold of his arms. All the time she continued shouting and screaming.

Suddenly, it was over. Luz had won the match. Her fellow passengers howled noisily, as did the uniformed men and the other spectators. They wanted more. When they saw that Luz's adversary was no longer resisting, they shouted at him to go on. But he refused.

One of the men walked over to the tangled pair, and good naturedly tapped Luz on the shoulder. *"Basta, señora, basta,"* he said. But she would not budge until he convinced her that she and Arturo Escutia would be safe. Only then did Luz agree to move from her vantage point. It took several men to assist her back to her feet.

The loser struggled to get up, furious but so embarrassed that he disappeared into the darkness without even looking for the gun that had popped out of his hand when Luz had first assaulted him. As the crowd hurled catcalls and boos in the direction of the defeated man, his companion gave final clearance for the Salvadoran bus to continue on its way, but not before he took most of Arturo Escutia's money.

II

After the incident, Luz became the hero of the group. Her fellow passengers congratulated her for her bravery. Proud of their compañera, they fought over who would sit next to her during the last miles of the trip. The bus hummed with soft voices that told and retold how Luz had scared *la mierda* out of the greedy officials.

Arturo and Luz sat next to each other often. Once, during a lull when the other passengers dozed, she turned to Arturo. "Hijo, quién eres, y qué haces tan lejos de tu familia?"

Shy at first, Arturo did not immediately respond to Luz's question about who he was. But then he spoke in a low tone, almost whispering. "My story, Doña Luz, isn't too different from that of many others. I'm nineteen years old, but sometimes I feel very, very old. My father was an office worker. He worked in one of the city buildings, and even though it wasn't a high position, still, he and my mother were able to give their children a good life. We were three brothers. The three of us went to school because my mother and father worked hard, and when the time came, I was able to make it to the university.

"Last year, when I was in my first year of studies, I joined some of my companions who helped out the poor people of the barrios. At times we even ventured out of the city to assist the campesinos. We really didn't do terribly important things, Doña Luz. We simply collected food and blankets for them. Little things like that.

"We did that for a while. Then one day some men came to where we were. They began to push us around, calling us communists and troublemakers. Well, we pushed back. Suddenly they pulled out sticks from I don't know where. We had a big fight. We were taken to the police station and warned to stay out of trouble, but something strange happened to all of us. Suddenly, we wanted, more than ever, to help the poor.

"So we began to organize and join others who were doing the

same thing. We stood on street corners with placards in our hands, trying to have others join us and not let bullies push us around for no reason. We passed out flyers, and even asked for signatures on petitions where we asked that the government take care of the people. I think...no...I know that we really got into trouble when we began to encourage factory workers. We asked them to unite in an effort to have the *patrones* give them just a little bit more money to help when they or their families got sick. We encouraged laborers to say something about the conditions at work.

"I have to tell you that I was paying more attention to this than to my books and studies. But I wasn't the only one. The rest of my compañeros and compañeras were in it up to here." Arturo marked an invisible line across his throat. Luz was staring past him. Her gaze was riveted on a tiny speck on the window pane.

"And what did your mother *and* father say about all of this?"

"*Bueno*, a neighbor snitched, he told them that he had seen me in the plaza passing out papers with subversive writing on it. You can imagine what they both thought. My father talked to me, trying to persuade me not to see my friends anymore, and to concentrate on my classes. Now I wish with all my heart that I had listened to him!"

"And your mother? What did she say to you?"

"She was scared. We all knew how some people had disappeared from the streets without anyone knowing what had happened to them. I thought of that too, but something inside of me told me that what I was doing was important, so I kept meeting with my companions, and writing letters, and standing in the plaza talking to people about how bad things were in our country.

"Things became serious. Our group began to grow. Then the same type of people who had attacked us with sticks would come after us more frequently."

"Who were they? Soldiers? Policemen?"

"I don't know. Nobody knew. They didn't wear uniforms but they walked and acted like soldiers. You know what I mean? They were dressed like campesinos but their bodies told us that they were trained to handle sticks, almost as if they had been rifles. Well, anyway, these people often confronted us. They pushed us, and tore our signs, and they called us names. And everyday this became worse, and a lot of the compañeros were afraid. Some of them went away. I don't blame them. I should have done the same thing."

The muffled grinding of the engine caused Arturo to stop talking.

"Then our group worked up the courage to organize a demonstration. We were convinced that if all of us who thought the same way gathered in public, showing our solidarity, then the government would respect our wishes. ¡Qué estúpidos! We went ahead and planned the demonstration. It was incredible! Many people had said that no one would show up, that most of the men and women of our country were satisfied with their lives, or that they were afraid to do such a thing. But they were wrong. You should have seen how many..."

"I remember all that. It was last July, wasn't it? I didn't go because I was afraid, but my comadre Aurora who always sticks her nose into everything did. She told me about it."

"Yes, it was last July. People came from everywhere. They came from the fields, and they joined hands with unionists and factory workers, shopkeepers, mechanics, teachers, clerks, housewives. Even their children came. I thought my heart was going to explode! I was so happy, and proud!

"We gathered at Plaza Barrios with our banners, and we carried signs that asked for justice and opportunity. When the students at the head gave the signal, I looked behind me, and there were so many people that I couldn't see even a little piece of the pavement.

"We began our march, and someone began shouting the word '*¡Justicia! ¡Libertad!*' We all imitated that voice, and the words became like thunder. '*¡Justicia! ¡Libertad! ¡Justicia!*' I remember that our voices sounded like one, bouncing off the walls and windows and doorways."

"I wonder what I would have done if I had been there?"

"I know you, Doña Luz. Perdón, I think I know you. You would have joined us. It was beautiful.

"Then, without warning, shooting began. At first, I thought that balloons were popping, but then I heard people screaming in terror! Something made me look up just in time to see that there were soldiers hiding in the rooftops of the taller buildings. They were everywhere. They crouched in the arches, behind pillars, and they were shooting into the crowd! They didn't even have to aim because each bullet brought somebody down. Everyone began to shove and to run, trying to escape. Panic was everywhere."

Luz held her hands to her mouth, her face tense. "Just like at the archbishop's funeral!" she whispered.

"When the soldiers saw how terrified the people were, they became confident and came out of their hiding places. They stepped forward shooting without caring. I remember that bodies began to fall all around me. Some of them were hit by bullets, others were trampled by those trying to run. Soldiers chased those of us who were able to break loose. Like rats, we scrambled down streets, around corners, up alleyways. The soldiers were able to capture most of the group, especially the ones that fell or stumbled. The noise of the screaming and of the shooting deafened me.

"I ran, Doña Luz! Like a coward, I headed home because I couldn't think of anything else to do. I had nowhere else to go. When I reached my house, I barged in. I must have looked like I was crazy. I stumbled into the kitchen where they...my family...were just beginning to eat. The four of them looked at me, shocked, and their look struck me as being funny. I guess I was hysterical because I started to laugh! I laughed out loud, louder than I had ever laughed in my life. It became so bad that my father stood up and slapped me. Then I became quiet."

"¿Tu padre te pegó?"

"He had to hit me, and I was grateful. It was only then that I saw how afraid he and my mother were for me. They knew...don't ask me how...but they knew that I had been involved in something serious. What they didn't know...yet...was that it had turned into a massacre. Without a word, my father looked at the others as if telling them not to speak. With his hand, he told me to sit at my place.

"My mother served me a plate, but each mouthful that I ate stuck in my throat as if it were straw or a lump of clay. And I could tell that it was the same for the rest of the family. It was obvious that we were expecting to hear something, maybe footsteps, or even loud knocking at the door.

"But the days that followed were quiet. I didn't return to the university because I was afraid. I helped my mother with the housework, and in the evening I talked to my father of what I should do next. Then, on the fourth night.... Oh, Doña Luz, *fue terrible!*

"That night, as we were sitting at the table, the front door opened with a loud noise. Suddenly we were surrounded by men. Again, they were dressed like campesinos, but those eyes, those cruel eyes told us they were not from the fields. They carried weapons. My father stood, but they didn't give him time to speak. A bullet tore a big hole in his forehead."

"Arturo, perhaps it's best if you don't talk about this. I can tell you're living through it all over again."

"It happened so suddenly that none of us had time to even say a word. It was quiet, so quiet! My father had slumped onto the table face down. Blood was pouring out of him. We were paralyzed. Then, in the next minute, my two brothers and my mother were killed."

Luz had taken Arturo's hands in hers, and she was holding them against her breast. She didn't know what to say, so she pretended to be listening to the murmuring that had begun at the rear of the bus. Some passengers had awakened.

"¿Y tú? ¿Por qué no te mataron a ti?"

"They told me why they weren't going to kill me. At least, not yet! One of them said to me, '¡Cabrón! You're going to live so you can tell your friends what happens to filthy communists like you!' Then he put his hand into the blood that was covering the table, and he printed a name on the wall: '*¡El escuadrón!*'

"I was beaten into unconsciousness. When I woke up I found that I was almost buried in garbage. They had dumped me at El Playón. When I tried to move, I couldn't. My arms were broken. So were some of my ribs. My mouth was so swollen that I couldn't say a word, much less scream like I wanted to do. Some of my teeth–see, right here, I'm missing some–they were kicked out by those animals, and my eyes were puffed up. I could hardly see. When I looked up into the gray sky everything was blurred, but when I began to focus my eyes I saw vultures flying over me. I realized that dead bodies must have been stuck in the filth.

"I don't know how long I laid there thinking I was having a nightmare. But then I heard voices. In the beginning they were far way, like echoes. Then the sounds came closer until I was able to make out someone huddling over me. 'This one's alive. Help me with him.' I heard the words clearly, and I felt them dragging me from the rubble. From there, I was carried up into the mountains of Chalatenango.

"Even though my body got well, my heart was sick. I never spoke to anyone. I just thought of my mother and father and brothers. It had been my fault. I tried to pray, but I couldn't. Instead of the prayers I knew, the words turned nasty and mean, and I cursed God for having allowed me to live. I hated the vultures because they had not devoured me."

"No more, por favor! You're free now. Think of that. Up there, where we're going, you'll find a new life. You'll have children of your own, and that way, your mother and father will again live. Think of it. Their blood is in you, and it will live on in your children."

Arturo listened to what Luz was saying, but he let her understand that he wanted to finish his story. "When I was in the mountains several of the men asked me to join the guerrillas. They reminded me that I was a marked man, and that to think that I was free was a mistake. Sooner or later, the *escuadrón* would catch up with me. Even though I knew they were right, I couldn't join them. I didn't want to be part of anything or anyone. But in spite of this they let me stay with them for months until I was well enough to travel."

After he finished, neither one of them spoke. More than an hour passed while Luz pondered, thinking of Arturo's story and wondering about his plans.

"What are you going to do now?"

"I'm going...well, I thought I was going to Los Angeles. But now that my money is gone, I'll have to stay in Mexico City, find work, and save for the next leg of the trip."

"Why Los Angeles? Who do you know there?"

Arturo wrinkled his forehead showing his uncertainty. "A friend of mine used to write to me from there. He told me he found work, and that there were others like me who also were working..."

His words stopped abruptly. Luz waited for him to finish, but he was quiet. She asked, "Do you have his address?"

"No!" Arturo's unexpectedly terse response told Luz that he had become annoyed by her inquiries. She regretted her manner, realizing that she had unwittingly become an intruder. She sat back in her seat silently mulling over an idea that began to take shape in her mind. However, her thoughts were cut short.

"And you, Señora, where are you going, and why?"

This turn in the conversation disconcerted Luz. Arturo's question uncannily echoed her own, and she felt intimidated to have someone else utter it out loud.

"I'm looking for my son. But I don't know where to search. I thought that I would begin by heading north... ." Her voice trailed off weakly, shaking nervously.

Arturo blushed. "Forgive me." Both were quiet for a moment, then he said, "I can't imagine what my mother would do if she were in your place."

After this, they withdrew into their thoughts.

The journey to Mexico City took another two days. Once, the trip was interrupted when the water pump of the bus broke down. Other times torrential rains that had come early in the season forced them to pull over to the side of the road. The vehicle was stopped frequently by police or by customs officers or by immigration authorities. Each time the passengers' pockets became emptier, and their possessions more meager.

During the tedious hours of the trip, Luz's mind drifted. She toyed with the idea of remaining with Arturo while they were both in Mexico City. Other times she even thought of going with him to Los Angeles. She imagined herself speaking to Bernabé. "I wonder what you would tell me to do, Hijo?" She thought also of the other son, the one taken from her by the Delcanos. She hardly knew anything about him, except that he had been educated, and that he held an important position in the government.

Whenever she thought of her first child, her mind filled with questions and premonitions. "I wonder what he looks like. Is he a good man? Surely he is. And even though he doesn't know me, he must think of me just as I think of him. He's probably married, and his children have my blood in their veins. When I told Arturo that his mother's blood would run in his children's body, I thought of my two sons. They are both a part of me. Even the one I don't know."

These reflections saddened Luz. To distract herself she focused on her surroundings. She looked around and wondered about her companions. What exactly had made them leave their land? Luz felt a tenderness towards each of them, sensing that, like her, none had really wanted to leave El Salvador. Like her, also, they might be wondering about what lay ahead.

"Doña Luz, you are talking to yourself. Are you feeling sick? Here, have a sip."

Luz was startled. Arturo's words jerked her out of her reverie. She had not realized that she was thinking out loud, and that others could hear her fears emerging from her heart.

The mud-spattered bus arrived in Mexico City in the late afternoon during peak traffic hours. The vehicle was forced to make its way slowly through Tlalpan, the southern edge of the city. Soon the passengers were overwhelmed by what they saw. Never had they imagined the jungle of cement and steel that awaited them in Mexico City. Their ears were bombarded by the blasting of car horns and vendors peddling newspapers, sarapes, chiclets and tortas. People were everywhere. The passengers felt their lungs and noses fill up with the city's dense smog. Their eyes started to run and to fill with tears. They look with amazement at the buildings and at the massive concrete walls grayed by a sooty coating. They pointed at tree trunks blackened and gnarled by pollution. Around them they saw men and women running and skittering from one side of the street to the other, dodging cars, buses and trucks. The streets and parks were filled with movement, and the campesinos and campesinas stared at elegantly dressed individuals who walked alongside other people in rags. Scrawny children and famished dogs scrambled over the sidewalks. In their hearts, the new arrivals felt fear in that city, overwhelmed by its size, movement, and sound.

At the end of the line, as the bus turned into Estación Taxqueña, Luz felt a lump forming in the pit of her stomach. She knew that the time had come for her to make a decision as to what she would do next in her search for her son Bernabé.

III

Most of the passengers planned to continue north but others, forced to stay in Mexico City because they had run short of money, began their farewells as soon as they got off the bus. Luz stood on the fringe of the bustling group staring vacantly around her. The cardboard box that held her things was on the pavement next to her feet. She had reached the end of the line, and she felt lost. At that moment Arturo approached her attempting an awkward goodbye.

"Bueno, Doña Luz, hasta la próxima..."

"Wait a minute!"

She gazed into his eyes with an intensity that made him shuffle nervously. Different thoughts were flashing through Luz's mind: Arturo wanted to reach Los Angeles, but didn't have the money. She had money, but not enough for the both of them. He had to stay in Mexico City, and her ticket took her only to Mexico City. He was alone, and she didn't want to be alone.

Luz walked to a nearby bench taking her box with one hand and Arturo's arm with the other one. She sat down and motioned him to join her. She paused to look around as she absorbed the disappointment stamped on the faces of so many people. From the way a man on her right was embracing his children, Luz sensed they were soon to be parted. In front of her was a woman whose stooped head betrayed her loneliness.

Luz was quiet for a long time before she spoke. "Arturo, look around us! Everywhere there's sadness because people are separating from each other. You lost your money because I fought with the official. At least, I think that's why he took your money."

"No. That's not the reason. He would have taken it anyway."

"Well, maybe. Anyway, let me speak. I haven't told you that when I began my trip I really didn't know where I was going. All I knew was that I was looking for my son. Why did I head for Mexico City? I wasn't sure of that either. Perhaps it was because in my heart

I hoped he would be doing what you are doing: heading north."

Luz sighed deeply. She was aware that Arturo was listening intently. "Now that I've reached this city, things have become a little bit clearer for me." Suddenly shifting her body to face Arturo she said, "Hijo, I want to go to Los Angeles. I think that maybe I'll find Bernabé there. Let me go with you."

Arturo jerked his head showing surprise. He was about to speak when Luz put her hand to his mouth. "I don't think I have enough money to go to Los Angeles right away. But even if I did, I don't want to go alone. So, let's stay here together, Arturo. I'll help you save money, and then we'll make our way up there. What do you say?"

He was smiling but his eyes contradicted his lips. Luz thought she understood and said, "Don't worry, Arturo. I can take care of myself. I won't be a burden."

He fastened his gaze on his feet. "I know you can take care of yourself. That's not it." Then looking at her he said, "Doña Luz, I hear Los Angeles is a big city."

"¿Y qué? So is Mexico City."

"Chances are that it will be impossible for you to find... ."

"I know! I know!" Luz was irked by the reality of his words. "But I must do it, Arturo, or else I'll stop breathing."

Arturo looked at her for a while. Then he smiled broadly as he shook his head in affirmation. Encouraged by this sudden turn, Luz rose to her feet, straightening her rumpled dress. She looked around as if searching for someone in particular. After a few minutes her eyes rested on a man, and motioning to Arturo to follow her, she approached the stranger. The man wore simple trousers, a white shirt, huaraches, and a straw sombrero which he carried in rough brown hands.

"Buenas tardes, Señor. May I speak to you for a moment?"

The man wrinkled his forehead in surprise but, with a smile, he responded, "Como no, Señora."

"Señor, this is my friend, Arturo Escutia."

Both men shook hands.

"Señor, as you probably can tell, we've come a long way...and we, well...we were wondering if you know..."

"You're from the south, aren't you?"

"Yes."

"And you need to find work so you can buy a ticket to finish your trip."

"Are there many like us?"

"Yes. Many."

The man gave them instructions on how to go to a laundry owned by a Spaniard. They would find the business in Colonia Cuauhtémoc, a district not far from the station. There, the man told Luz and Arturo, they would find temporary work.

"Muchas gracias, Señor, y hasta luego."

"¡Para servirles, Senora!"

Turning to Arturo, Luz said, "*¡Vámonos!*" as she tugged at his sleeve.

"But Doña Luz, why should we believe this man? How do we know he is telling the truth?"

"I know in my heart it's the truth. Now, let's go, Arturo. Every minute is important."

Luz picked up her belongings and Arturo followed her as she headed for the exit. When they walked through the wide doors of the station into a milling crowd, Luz instructed Arturo to ask someone how to find Colonia Cuauhtémoc; she would do the same.

No one paid attention to Luz or Arturo; they were pushed aside or ignored. A few passersby shook their head negatively, others muttered unintelligible words. Finally a man, after taking a long pause to look in several directions, pointed towards the city's eastern district. Neither Luz nor Arturo questioned the instructions, and picking up their bundles, they walked for nearly an hour until Luz, fatigued and breathing heavily, stopped suddenly.

"Arturo, I have a strange feeling. Something tells me that this isn't the way to the laundry. Look. It's alomost dark. Even if we did find the place I'm sure no one would be there now. We'd better think of something else to do."

"Let's go back to the station and spend the night there."

Luz and Arturo returned to the terminal in search of a bench or vacant corner in which to sleep but the station was jammed with transients and weary travelers who eyed one another suspiciously. The scramble for space was made more difficult by the station guards who shooed away anyone who looked like an overnighter. To evade the watchmen, those people searching for a place pretended to be waiting for a bus while they snatched short spurts of sleep.

"Hijo, we'll have to sleep standing up. There's nothing else to do. Tomorrow will come soon, and things will be better."

Next day, as daylight filtered through the city's thick layer of smoke and fog, Luz and Arturo began their search. This time Luz was intent on not burning her energy following ill-given instructions. By noon, she and Arturo had found their way to the laundry.

The owner of Lavandería La Regenta provided work for Luz and Arturo without questions, and even though it turned out that the wages were low, the work hours were regular. In the beginning Luz, who had only washed clothes by hand, felt intimidated by the oversized machine she was instructed to operate. But she forced herself to overcome her fears by following the instructions given by the owner, even though the machine's grinding noises rattled her nerves.

Arturo, who was assigned to be a helper on the laundry's delivery truck, had to deal with the weakness he still felt in his arms and legs. But like Luz, he too forced himself to forget everything and do his work. He liked the job because it took him deep into the city, where he felt sheltered by anonymity.

Luz and Arturo found a room in Colonia Cuauhtémoc the same day they landed their jobs. The accommodations were meager. The room provided only two cots along with a nightstand and a kitchenette, but they were grateful because they had a place to stay when they were not working. Together they began to save the few *pesos* that remained after they paid rent and bought food.

In the beginning, saving money was especially hard because they and other Central Americans were routinely hunted out by Mexican immigration agents. The harassment posed by the agents of *la Migra,* who sniffed out the foreigners' telltale timidity, was constant and efficient. The pattern was always the same.

"Nombre y documentos, por favor."

Money seemed to be the only thing that mattered to the immigration agents, and like the other workers, Luz and Arturo frequently found themselves cornered by them and forced to produce whatever *pesos* they had. Once, Arturo had to hide an entire day in a post office while a patrol car cruised the district. As a result, he was docked a full day's wages.

Luz was frustrated by the intimidation, for she felt that the prospect of reaching Los Angeles was slipping away. She could think of nothing else to do, however; so, she resorted to tricks such as crying out loud, then shouting that she was a poor, solitary, penniless woman who wanted to be friends with the mexicanos while she spent a short time in their land. Even though it worked a few times, Luz decided to abandon this tactic because she realized it only embarrassed the officials into leaving her alone, and she feared they would pick on her even more out of spite.

She decided to try another way. Luz began by offering gifts of food or drink as a substitute for the money demanded by the agents. She also approached them as if they had been her friends for years, using words and tones she had picked up from fellow Mexican workers.

"¿Qué tal, mi sargento? Beautiful day, isn't it? All of you here are so lucky. No wonder everyone in the world loves you. Here, try this little nothing that I made for you today. How's the family? I hear you have a beautiful wife and intelligent kids."

These words were always followed by Luz's loud, contagious laughter. The ploy not only worked once or twice; its effects lasted. Soon those men looked for Luz among the piles of soiled sheets and pillowcases, not for her money, but for her food and flattery, and her loud laughter. Her success with offering food to *la Migra* made Luz think about peddling food to her fellow workers. She started a small business and soon she and Arturo were able to begin saving for their trek north.

They lived in Mexico City for more than a year, working every day except Sundays. When they finally had enough *pesos* to buy their tickets to Tijuana and to pay for the coyote who would guide them across the border into the United States, they felt they were ready to leave Mexico City. On the day their bus left the terminal at dawn, Luz and Arturo were so filled with anxiety that neither dared to share this with the other.

IV

Luz and Arturo arrived at the Tijuana bus terminal forty hours later, exhausted and bloated from sitting in their cramped seat. As soon as they stepped out of the bus, they were approached by a woman who asked them if they wanted to cross the border that night. Without waiting for an answer, she told them she could be their guide. The price was five hundred American dollars apiece.

Luz stared at the woman for a few moments, caught off guard by the suddenness of what was happening. More than her words, it was the woman's appearance that held Luz's attention. She was about thirty-five. Old enough, Luz figured, to have experience in her business. The woman was tall and slender, yet her body conveyed a muscular strength that gave Luz the impression that she would be able to lead them across the border.

The coyota returned Luz's gaze, evidently allowing time for the older woman to make up her mind. She took a step closer to Luz, who squinted as she concentrated on the woman's face. Luz regarded her dark skin and high forehead, and the deeply set eyes that steadily returned her questioning stare. With a glance, she took in the coyota's faded levis and plaid shirt under a shabby sweatshirt, and her eyes widened when she saw the woman's scratched, muddy cowboy boots. She had seen only men wear such shoes.

Luz again looked into the woman's eyes. She was tough, and Luz knew that she had to drive a hard bargain. She began to cry. "¡Señora, por favor! Have a heart! How can you charge so much? We're poor people who have come a long way. Where do you think we can find so many dólares? All we have is one hundred dollars to cover the two of us. Please! For the love of your mamacita!"

The woman crossed her arms over her chest and laughed out loud as she looked into Luz's eyes. She spoke firmly. "Señora, I'm not in the habit of eating fairy tales for dinner. You've been in Mexico City for a long time. I have eyes, don't I? I can tell that you're not starving. Both of you have eaten a lot of enchiladas and tacos. Just look at those nalgas!"

She gave Luz a quick, hard smack on her behind. Then, ignoring the older woman's look of outrage, the coyota continued to speak rapidly. "Look, Señora. Just to show you that I have feelings, I'll consider guiding the both of you at the reduced rate of seven hundred dollars. Half now; the rest when I get you to Los Angeles. Take it or leave it!"

Luz knew that she was facing her match. She answered with one word. "Bueno."

The coyota led them to a man who was standing nearby. He was wearing a long overcoat, inappropriate for the sultry weather in Tijuana. The coat had a purpose though, for it concealed deep inner pockets which were filled with money. The coyota pulled Luz nearer to the man, then whispered into her ear. "This man will change your *pesos* into American dollars. A good rate, I guarantee."

When Arturo began to move closer, the coyota turned on him. "You stay over there!"

Arturo obeyed.

Even though she felt distrust, Luz decided that she and Arturo had no alternative. However, she needed to speak with him, so she pulled him to the side. "Hijo, we're taking a big chance. We can be robbed, even killed. Remember the stories we've been hearing since we left home. But what can we do? We need someone to help us get across, so what does it matter if it's this one, or someone else? What do you say?"

Arturo agreed with her. "Let's try to make it to the other side. The sooner the better. I think you made a good bargain. We have the money, don't we?"

"With a little left over for when we get to Los Angeles."

Before they returned to where the others were waiting, she turned to a wall. She didn't want anyone to see what she was doing. Luz withdrew the amount of *pesos* she estimated she could exchange for a little more than seven hundred American dollars. She walked over to the money vendor, and no sooner had the man placed the green bills on her palm, then she heard the coyota's sharp voice. "Three hundred and fifty dollars, por favor!"

She signaled Luz and Arturo to follow her to a waiting car. They went as far as Mesa Otay, the last stretch of land between Mexico and California. There, the coyota instructed them to wait until it got dark. Finally, when Luz could barely see her hand in front of her, the woman gave the signal. "¡Vámonos!"

They walked together under the cover of darkness. As Luz and Arturo trekked behind the woman, they sensed that they were not alone, that other people were also following. Suddenly someone issued a warning, "¡La Migra! ¡Cuidado!" The coyota turned with unexpected speed, and murmured one word, "¡Abajo!"

All three fell to the ground, clinging to it, melting into it, hoping that it would split open so that they could crawl into its safety. Unexpectedly a light flashed on. Like a giant eye, it seemed to be coming from somewhere in the sky, slowly scanning the terrain. No one moved. All that could be heard were the crickets and the dry grass rasping in the mild breeze. The light had not detected the bodies crouched behind bushes and rocks. It flashed out as suddenly as it had gone on.

"¡Vámonos!" The coyota was again on her feet and moving. They continued in the dark for hours over rough, rocky terrain. The coyota was sure footed but Luz and Arturo bumped into rocks and tripped over gopher holes. Luz had not rested or eaten since she had gotten off the bus. She was fatigued but she pushed herself fearing she would be left behind if she stopped. Arturo was exhausted too, but he knew that he still had reserves of energy, enough for himself and Luz.

Dawn was breaking as they ascended a hill. Upon reaching the summit, they were struck with awe at the sight that spread beneath their feet. Their heavy breathing stopped abruptly as their eyes glowed in disbelief. Below, even though diffused by dawn's advancing light, was an illuminated sea of streets and buildings. A blur of neon formed a mass of light and color, edged by a highway that was a ribbon of liquid silver. Luz and Arturo wondered if fatigue had caused their eyes to trick them because as far as they could see there was brilliance, limited only in the distance by a vast ocean. To their left, they saw the lights of San Diego unfolding beneath them, and their hearts stopped when they realized that farther north, where their eyes could not see, was their destination.

Without thinking, Luz and Arturo threw their arms around one another and wept.

V

The lights of San Diego receded behind them. The coyota had guided Luz and Arturo over an inland trail, taking them past the U.S. Immigration station at San Onofre, and then down to connect with the highway. A man in a car was waiting for them a few yards beyond Las Pulgas Road on California Interstate 5.

The driver got out of the car as they approached, extending a rough hand first to Luz, and then to Arturo. "Me llamo Ordaz."

Ordaz turned to the coyota and spoke in English. His words were casual, as if he had seen her only hours before. "You're late. I was beginning to worry."

"The old bag slowed me down."

The coyota spoke to the man in English, knowing that her clients were unable to understand her. Then, she switched to Spanish to introduce herself to Luz and Arturo. "Me llamo Petra Traslaviña. I was born back in San Ysidro on a dairy farm. I speak English and Spanish."

There was little talk among them beyond this first encounter. The four piled into a battered Pontiac station wagon, and with Ordaz at the wheel, they headed north. The woman pulled out a pack of Mexican cigarettes, smoking one after the other, until Ordaz started to cough. He opened the window complaining, "Por favor, Petra, you wanna choke us to death?"

"Shut up!" she retorted rapidly, slurring the English *sh*.

The phrase engraved itself in Luz's memory. She liked the sound of it. She liked its effect even more, since she noticed that Ordaz was silenced by the magical phrase. Inwardly, Luz practiced her first English words, repeating them over and again under her breath.

Luz and Arturo were quiet during the trip mainly because they were frightened by the speed at which Ordaz was driving. As she looked out over the coyota's shoulder, Luz knew that she didn't like what she was feeling and hearing. She even disliked the smell of the air, and she felt especially threatened by the early morning fog.

When the headlights of oncoming cars broke the grayness, her eyes squinted with pain.

The hours seemed endless, and they were relieved when Ordaz finally steered the Pontiac off the freeway and onto the streets of Los Angeles. Like children, Luz and Arturo looked around, craning their necks, curiously peering through the windows and seeing that people waited for their turn to step onto the street. Luz thought it was silly the way those people moved in groups. No one ran out onto the street, leaping, jumping, dodging cars as happened in Mexico City and back home. Right away, she missed the vendors peddling wares, and the stands with food and drink.

Suddenly, Luz was struck by the thought that she didn't know where the coyota was taking them. As if reading Luz's mind, the woman asked, "Do you have a place you want me to take you to?"

Rattled by the question, Luz responded timidly. "No. We didn't have time to think."

"I thought so. It's the same with all of you."

The coyota was quiet for a while before she whispered to Ordaz, who shook his head in response. They engaged in a heated exchange of words in English, the driver obviously disagreeing with what the coyota was proposing. Finally, seeming to have nothing more to say, Ordaz shrugged his shoulders, apparently accepting defeat. The coyota turned to her passengers.

"Vieja, I know of a place where you two can find a roof and a meal until you find work. But..." She was hesitating. "¡Mierda!...just don't tell them I brought you. They don't like me because I charge you people money."

What she said next was muttered and garbled. Luz and Arturo did not understand her so they kept quiet, feeling slightly uneasy and confused. By this time Ordaz was on Cahuenga Boulevard in Hollywood. He turned up a short street, and pulled into the parking lot of Saint Turibius Church, where the battered wagon spurted, then came to a stand-still.

"Hasta aquí. You've arrived."

The coyota was looking directly at Luz, who thought she detected a warning sign in the woman's eyes. "It was easy this time, Señora. Remember, don't get caught by *la Migra,* because it might not be so good the next time around. But if that happens, you know that you can find me at the station in Tijuana."

Again, the coyota seemed to be fumbling for words. Then she

said, "Just don't get any funny ideas hanging around these people. I mean, they love to call themselves voluntarios, and they'll do anything for nothing. Yo no soy así. I'll charge you money all over again, believe me!"

The coyota seemed embarrassed. Stiffly, she shifted in her seat, pointing at a two-story, Spanish-style house next to the church.

"See that house?"

Luz nodded.

"Bueno. Just walk up to the front door, knock, and tell them who you are, and where you're from. They'll be good to you. But, as I already told you, don't mention me."

She turned to Arturo. "Take care of yourself, Muchacho. I've known a few like you who have gotten themselves killed out there."

With her chin, she pointed toward the street. When Arturo opened his mouth to speak, the coyota cut him off curtly. "My three hundred and fifty dollars, por favor."

She stretched out her hand in Luz's direction without realizing that her words about other young men who resembled Arturo had had an impact on Luz. "Petra, have you by any chance met my son? His name is Bernabé and he looks like this young man."

The coyota looked into Luz's eyes. When she spoke her voice was almost soft. "They all look like Arturo, Madre. They all have the same fever in their eyes. How could I possibly know your son from all the rest?"

Luz's heart shuddered when the coyota called her madre. Something told her that the woman did know Bernabé. This thought filled her with new hope, and she gladly reached into her purse. She put the money into the coyota's hand, saying, "Hasta pronto. I hope, Petra, that our paths will cross again sooner or later."

Luz and Arturo were handed the small bundles they had brought with them from Mexico City. As they stepped out of the car, the engine cranked on, backfiring loudly. When it disappeared into the flow of traffic, both realized that even though only three days had passed since they left Mexico, they had crossed over into a world unknown to them. They were aware that they were facing days and months, perhaps even years, filled with dangers neither of them could imagine.

Feeling apprehensive they were silent as they approached the large house that their guide had pointed out. They didn't know that the building had been a convent and that it was now a refuge run by priests and other volunteers. Neither realized that they were entering a sanctuary for the displaced and for those without documents or jobs. When they were shown in, Luz and Arturo were surprised at how warmly they were received. No one asked any questions. Afterwards, they were given food to eat and a place to sleep.

VI

Casa Andrade, an extension of Saint Turibius Parish, was a mix of immigrants and refugees who had made their way to the United Stated from Mexico and Central America. The house was many things: temporary home, town hall, and information center. Neither Luz nor Arturo had ever experienced such an amalgam of people. Both of them listened intently to their new companions as they jabbered in different accents telling how they had arrived in Los Angeles. At the end of each story almost all of them spoke of the rumors they had heard about life in Los Angeles, about the city's massiveness and the difficulties of living there.

Luz gradually began to understand the vastness of the place into which she and Arturo had ventured, and she saw that even if Bernabé were in the city, the probability of her ever seeing him was unlikely. The weight of this thought bore down on Luz, saddening her. Her dejection was intensified by her new surroundings. She had never lived under the same roof with so many people, some of them crowded into rooms according to families, age or sex. Even though she spoke the same language and shared many of their experiences, Luz felt that she was a stranger. She also felt awkward because even though the staff was kind, she knew that the food and shelter she was receiving was charity. Luz had always worked for her keep, and she found her stay at Casa Andrade difficult to accept.

She tried to compensate by helping out in the kitchen or by watching children who had no one to care for them or by cleaning the house. But nothing helped to dispel her feeling of dependency. Luz also struggled with a nagging sense of floundering, of hanging in suspension, of waiting for something to happen, yet not knowing, when or what it would be. She missed her home city, and as the days drifted by, her heart seemed to sink into numbness.

Events at Casa Andrade, however, were teeming with similar disappointments and disillusionments. Luz was dismayed to see that she was not the only one who had lost her son. Letters and notes were posted daily. They told of children, wives, husbands and friends who had disappeared in the upheaval taking place in El Salvador. In the evening, one or two people would meet with Luz for a cup of coffee. They would discuss how matters back home were becoming worse by the day. To return to that country, they affirmed, would mean certain punishment, maybe even death.

Luz turned to Arturo to see what was on his mind, but she soon realized that he was not experiencing her shakiness. Instead she found that he had gained confidence during their few days at Casa Andrade.

"Doña Luz, I haven't changed my mind" he said. "I'm going ahead with my plan. I'm staying. One of the compañeros here told me that he's found a job, and that maybe there's a place for me. After that I'll be able to pay rent for a place to live."

She mulled over her situation for several days as she went about her chores. Luz had worked in Mexico City, and she had saved money. She had made new acquaintances there, and she had not been unhappy. Why shouldn't she expect the same thing to happen in Los Angeles? Maybe she and Arturo could share a place again.

Luz was thinking about her recent past, as the shelter began to buzz with news. The son of Doña Elena Marín, a refugee housed in Casa Andrade, had just been killed by government soldiers in El Salvador. What made this latest death exceptional was that the young man had been a volunteer worker at the shelter. Gilberto Marín had arrived in Los Angeles years before his mother, and had distinguished himself among the staff by his dedication to the refugees who stayed at the house. Shortly after Doña Elena arrived at the sanctuary, the young man volunteered to return to El Salvador to help others escape to Los Angeles. And now one of the house workers had heard that he had been killed while attempting to escape the country.

The staff members of Casa Andrade were stunned by the loss of their companion. In a place where news of losses and deaths was almost a daily occurrence, the murder of a co-worker, nonetheless, was shocking. The entire staff, as well as the parish priests, met for a long session behind closed doors. Even though the refugees did not know what had been discussed, the grief of each member of the staff was evident when they came out of the meeting.

The day after the community of Casa Andrade and the parish congregation had been told about the death of Gilberto, they all attended a memorial mass for him. A silent grief engulfed the church. Hardly anyone wept, but there was profound sorrow stamped on the face of those men and women. Several priests approached Doña Elena during the service, reassuring her and speaking in praise of her son's generosity and dedication. Finally, at the end of the mass, as part of the homage, the name of the shelter was changed to Casa Gilberto, in memory of the young man.

After that night, Luz stayed close to Doña Elena, barely speaking to her but showing how earnestly she identified with her. The mother's grief clung to Luz, penetrating her, becoming part of her, and as the days passed, she reflected with even more intensity on her own situation, and the whereabouts of Bernabé.

Luz was in the midst of this personal turmoil when the community was stunned by further news regarding Gilberto. To everyone's confusion, a rumor spread from person to person saying that the initial report of the young man's death had been a mistake. He was alive, and on his way to Los Angeles.

This turn of events disconcerted the people of the shelter. Some thought it was a joke. Others said that someone was trying to give Doña Elena a new, but false hope. Casa Gilberto buzzed with doubting voices. No one knew what to make of what they had heard. Finally, one of the priests convened everyone in the church hall and calmly relayed the report that the news of Gilberto's death had been based on mistaken information. The young man was alive.

The priest's words were followed by an initial gasp from the crowd. Then, someone began to clap, and finally they gave each other back slaps and hugs as they cheered loudly. When they turned to look at Doña Elena, however, they saw that she was so shocked she was almost passing out. Several men and women reached out to her, propping her against one of the pillars until she was helped to her room by other women.

Luz didn't know how to react. Her hands had grown cold and her heart was beating so fast that her breath came in spurts. She felt pulled in different directions, relieved that Gilberto was alive after all, but filled with frustration and outrage on behalf of his mother who had lived through the pain of thinking she had lost her son. Luz felt an irresistible urge to confront the priest who had given them the news in such a matter-of-fact manner. She yearned to slap his face or to insult the members of the staff who were standing by, foolishly gawking. She wanted to lash out in indignation. Gilberto's mother had suffered unspeakably, and all because of a blunder committed by one of them.

Realizing that she was losing a grip on herself, Luz went to the room where she sat in the dark for a long while. A few hours later she went to the woman's room. Luz found her ashen-faced, but in control of herself.

"Doña Elena, I don't know what to say to you. How cruel... ."

"Please don't feel sorry for me," the woman quickly responded. "He's alive. That is all that matters."

Luz didn't speak any more. She couldn't. Instead she sat next to Doña Elena for a long time, grappling with the rage she was still feeling. What was happening to them all, she wondered. Would she be able to continue to live in such a state of uncertainty? Would she be able to survive a life that had left her so shattered and confused?

During the days that followed, her anger subsided and for several nights Luz meditated on Doña Elena's words. Putting herself in her place, she thought of the joy she would feel if Bernabé were to enter her life again. Yes, her pain and anxieties would be erased. Everything else would be forgotten if only he were to return. Luz again yearned to renew the search for her son, but she remained calm. Finally, she realized how unlikely it was that she would find him.

Coming to terms with this realization made it easier for her to approach Arturo once more. "Hijo, what if you and I find a place to live? I'll work. I'm still strong."

He didn't hesitate this time and appeared relieved. Putting his arm around her shoulders, Arturo drew Luz close to him. "We have to stay here for the time being," he reassured her. "Here we'll be safe."

VII

Los Angeles-October 1989.

Arturo found a job changing tires in an auto shop and, soon after, he and Luz moved into a small apartment. She began to earn her living by cleaning houses during the week, but on Saturday and Sunday she helped out in the church kitchen, preparing food for the new arrivals. Over the years Luz became an essential part of Casa Andrade. Her contagious laughter echoed in the hallways, and her words of consolation and encouragement often helped to dispel the anxieties of the growing number of refugees who knocked at the doors of Saint Turibius.

One late evening, as the sun's waning rays filtered through the west windows of their apartment, Luz and Arturo were conversing about their work at Casa Andrade. The sounds of cars and pedestrians had quieted down, and the white curtains listlessly floated back and forth in the breeze of the early night. Without a warning, the front door suddenly crashed open, and five men burst into the apartment. They rushed to where Luz and Arturo were sitting. Two of them had handkerchiefs over their faces. The others wore Halloween masks, rubbery, grotesque visages.

It happened so quickly that Luz and Arturo were stunned. They froze in their seats, paralyzed with fear. Seconds seemed an eternity, and Luz's eyes bulged with terror and incomprehension, while her lips quivered in an attempt to utter words that stuck in her throat. Sickened by the masked faces, she began to vomit. White liquid squeezed out the sides of her mouth. Arturo grasped what was happening sooner than Luz. Springing forward, he attempted to resist the attack by thrusting his body, arms outstretched, towards the intruders. But it was useless. The men grabbed his arms and legs, twisting and pulling at each limb. Luz heard the crunch of bones and moaning that spilled from Arturo's lips, but the shouting of his attackers was drowning out his cries.

"¡Cabrón!"

"¡Hijo de tu puta madre!"

"¡Que te joda el diablo!"

Their hoarse insults and screams were soon drowned out by the blasts of rapid gunfire. The explosions filling the air canceled out everything for Luz. They erased thought, destroyed feeling, killed all hope. It took only seconds, and in that brief interval, Luz understood the speed of smoke and fire. Her eyes relayed to her brain the efficiency with which a gun can kill. She was blinded by the flames jetting out of the assassins' weapons as they pumped death into Arturo's body. For Luz, the shots that spilled from those guns were the split tongues of snakes, lethal and poisonous, and their spewing was devouring Arturo, taking him from her. She witnessed Arturo being butchered as if he were a pig or a rabid dog.

Then the detonations stopped, and as abruptly as they had appeared, the intruders abandoned the apartment. When the grayish smoke lifted to the ceiling, Luz found herself alone. She sat on the floor, her legs stretched forward, rigidly spread apart as she held Arturo's body in her arms. Her elbows dripped with blood, and she moaned and wept, as she rocked back and forth on her haunches. Momentarily stunned out of her mind, Luz let out a lament, a mournful cradle song for a dead son. As she hummed, she stared straight ahead, her blank eyes riveted on the bloody hand print tattooed on the white wall.

When the police entered Luz's apartment, it was difficult for them to process what had taken place. Rounds of machine gun bullets were extracted from the walls, ceiling and floor but the investigators were unable to come up with logical reasons for the brutality or to understand why the man had been senselessly slaughtered while the woman had gone unharmed. Their questions remained unanswered, and the police had only Luz's mute stare and slouched body with which to contend because she was unable to speak. The police were left to decipher the evidence on their own: a room ripped to shreds by gun fire, the body of a young man nearly dismembered, and the enigma of a bloody hand print plastered on the wall.

"Tell us who did it."

"Señora, we can help if you tell us what you know."

"How many were they?"

"What did they look like?"

"Did they take anything of value?"

Luz responded to this question only. "They took my son Arturo."

When the news of Arturo's death hit Saint Turibius, the priests and several volunteers rushed to the police station to help Luz. The police explained that she had said very little. Since they were unable to extract any information from her beyond the name of her son, the investigators concluded that she had undergone a stroke, or perhaps a mental break-down, and she was taken to the County Hospital. Insofar as the crime was concerned, the report stated that the department was unwilling to accept the bloody hand print found at the scene as evidence. It was construed as a trick meant to mislead the investigation. The crime was officially recorded as gang related and designated to be pursued by normal channels.

During the hospital examination, Luz remained silent even though the police resumed their interrogation.

"Do the priests and those other people know who might have done this to your son?"

"Why are they insisting that your son's death was not gang related? What makes them say that, Señora?"

"If it wasn't the punks, then who in the Hell was it? And why?"

"Was your son on drugs? Did he peddle junk?"

"Your friends want to take you back to the church, but you understand that we can't allow that, don't you?"

Luz's general examination failed to disclose evidence of physical injuries or of a mental break-down, and she was released. Meanwhile, the police gave up on using her as a resource, so her case was turned over to the immigration authorities who submitted her to further questioning. She failed to answer the officials' questions regarding her documentation, and she was unable to provide proof of legal residency and was declared an illegal alien subject to immediate deportation.

Luz didn't care about what was happening to her because she had plummeted deep into a solitary world. After the police finished interrogating her, and the nurses and doctors finished probing her body, her soul fled. By the time the immigration agents asked for her papers, Luz's spirit had taken shelter in a niche that no one could find. Only she could hear herself speak.

"Bernabé, where are you, my son?"she kept asking. "Was it Arturo they killed, or was it you? And why is everything around me in ruins? Everything is black."

The priests of Casa Andrade and the staff did everything possible to have Luz released. They spent hours on the telephone, calling supporters who were influential with city officials and business people but nothing worked. Luz was indeed to be deported. She was taken to the detention center on a gray November day. Just before she boarded the bus that would take her to Tijuana, one of the Casa Andrade workers handed her a wad of dollar bills. "Buena suerte, Doña Luz. I hope our paths cross one day soon," he said.

As the bus sped southbound on the freeway, Luz was weeping, and mumbling under her breath. "I'll never return to this place of death," she swore to herself. "Never! Never! Arturo, my son, why did they kill you? Will they now be able to get away with your death?"

Luz paused, then went on, "And Bernabé, where are you? I swear I'll find you, my son. I will! And when I have you in my arms once more, we'll never, ever be separated again!"

VIII

Once on the road Luz stopped crying. As the bus increased its speed she gradually became calm. She sat straight, listening to her thoughts. Her mind reached back in time to the events of her trip north from El Salvador. Her thoughts were riveted on Arturo who unwittingly had helped her along the way. She was reliving many of their conversations, most of them still vividly echoing in her memory.

Then Arturo's image appeared. Inwardly she saw him. His face, however, was abruptly erased as she remembered the blast of gunfire which had snuffed out his life.

Luz was heading back in the direction from where she had come. Her hands were empty, for she was returning without Bernabé, and now she had also lost Arturo. Luz stared out the window of the bus vacantly, her eyes reflecting the California hillside interspersed with structures and billboards. Then, as the hours passed, she began to experience a strange sensation. She felt the grief that had thrashed her heart after Arturo's death subside. A growing distance between her body and spirit took hold of her, as if her soul were drifting away from pain, uniting itself to Arturo and to Bernabé.

Luz concentrated on her emotions attempting to sort them out, to grasp their meaning. After a while, she realized that she was finally returning to her source, her place of origin.

When the bus arrived in Tijuana, it stopped at the border on the American side, and its passengers were ordered to get off. As they straggled off the bus, pushing and bumping into one another, a U.S. agent steered the first person in the direction of the Mexican side of the border, and in a loud voice barked out his order.

"Get going!"

As the deportees shuffled towards the other side, they could hear the agents' laughter, and comments.

"Good riddance!"

"Oh, they'll be back. Wanna bet?"

"Wet-backs love a free ride."

Luz was mumbling. "¡Cabrones!" We leave our sweat and tears in your land, and all you can do is make fun of us."

Once off the bus she felt that her legs, numbed by the hours spent in the cramped bus seat, could barely support her. Her steps were hesitant and tottering at first, but as she regained her strength, she walked with more confidence. Even though she was still enshrouded by sadness, her reflections on the trip to the border had filled her with new determination.

She looked around searching for someone to give her information. Her eyes landed on a young woman. "Hija, dime dónde está la estación de camiones que van hacia el sur."

The girl informed Luz that the south-bound terminal was located in Mesa Otay.

"Bien. Muchas gracias."

As Luz moved through the crowds, she felt her strength returning. She looked around and hailed a taxi. As she stepped inside the car she smiled at the driver. "La camionera hacia el sur, por favor."

When she arrived at the station she was informed that the next bus was heading for Guatemala and El Salvador was scheduled to leave that evening at eight. After she purchased her ticket, she sat in the restaurant of the terminal waiting for the hours to pass. She thought of the people she had met; all of those with whom she had worked during the years of her search. She wondered if she would ever meet any of them again.

At seven-thirty, the station microphone clicked on. A nasal voice announced that the south-bound bus was beginning to load its passengers in the embarkation area. Making her way to the landing, Luz stepped gingerly onto the bus that would retrace her steps back to El Salvador. Once in her seat, she pushed the rusty window frame to one side, and as she looked out she saw a mass of faces beneath her. Some were smiling. Most of them, however, were etched with sadness. When the bus began to move, Luz leaned back in her seat. Her eyes were closed as she tried to summon up the image of her lost son. Would she ever see him again, she wondered as the bus headed south. She reflected on the pattern of her life. One after another, each of her sons had been taken from her, and there was nothing she could have done to prevent her loss.

PART THREE

...guerrillas and army troops battled in the capital on the second day of a guerrilla offensive that has left hundreds of dead and wounded...The weekend fighting between army troops and an estimated 1,000 guerrillas was the worst in 10 years of civil war.

Los Angeles Times, November 13, 1989

I

San Salvador, 1989.

"I left this city in search of my son because he disappeared years ago in these very streets, somewhere near the Cathedral. It happened on the day the Archbishop was buried. But now I've returned, my hands empty.

"Please don't think that I was careless in losing my son. Bernabé and I were among the mourners, but because he was carrying the cross in the procession, he was at the head, and I was behind him. Once the gun shots began we all turned like frightened cattle. There was a confusion that to this day I cannot describe. When we heard the explosions, we screamed and pushed, trying to escape. I kept my eyes on my son, but suddenly, he disappeared. At that same moment I was forced to my knees, and everything went black. I can't tell you how long I was in that stupor. When I came out of it, the street was empty except for the dead and a few weeping people. The rest had run away hoping to save their lives.

"All I could think of was my son but I didn't find him even though I ran through the streets shouting for him. I pounded on shuttered doors, screaming out his name, but no one had the courage to even stick their nose out the window. When I returned to the Cathedral hoping to find him, all I found were confused, lost people.

"'Have you seen my son?' I asked over and again, but they looked at me as if I had lost my mind. I remember that I turned to a woman who was sitting at the foot of the main altar, and I asked 'Have you seen my son?' I'll never forget her eyes. They were pools of black mud, empty, cold eyes, and she responded, 'You're looking for your son, and I'm sitting here waiting to die. I'm waiting to follow my babies. They all died today. A soldier shot each one in the head. You're looking for one son. I lost all four of mine.'

"Sí, Padre, it happened many years ago, but I haven't stopped looking for him. I didn't stay here in this city because everyone told me they thought that Bernabé would have taken a bus headed for *el norte*. Many young men did the same thing because they were afraid for their lives. So I followed. My journey has been long. I traveled first to Mexico, then to Los Angeles, and there I spent years hoping to find him. But I did not, so I came back to San Salvador only to find sighs and death and echoes of death. I've walked the streets for days, asking people if by chance they had ever seen my son. I went to Soyapango and found narrow streets and overgrown passageways clogged with dying people. When I went to Cuscatancingo to the church where my son used to assist at mass, I found men fighting with each other like enraged dogs. The church was in ruins, the statue of Our Lady was riddled with bullets, and the priest could not respond to my questions regarding Bernabé. His eyes were blank, like the eyes of a dead man. Then, when I made my way to Zacamil and to the Church of Christ Our Savior, I found a sign nailed to the door. It said, 'Do not enter. This is a mine field.' "

Luz Delcano was speaking rapidly in English and Spanish to a priest she barely knew, Father Hugh Joyce. He sat next to her, huddled on the cement floor of the shelter along with other men, women and children, most of them Salvadoran, who were there to escape the battle raging on the city streets between guerrillas and government troops.

"Padrecito maybe you've seen my son. He's not very tall. He is slim, and he has a beautiful face with eyes that are round and filled with light. His hair is brown, and not too curly. His hands are the hands of an artist, with small fingers. Did you ever run into him in Los Angeles? Someone told me that you're from Los Angeles, although I never saw you in our church on Sundays."

"Señora, I'm not from Los Angeles."

The woman's words were blurring in the priest's mind; several months of extreme fatigue were overtaking him, and he was struggling to keep awake. It was not for her sake, however, that he fought off his need to sleep, but because he was afraid of sleeping. He feared being left alone with thoughts and memories that nagged and harped, reminding him of what he wanted to forget. He had come to San Salvador hoping to be free of his nightmares, but he was afraid that if he fell asleep, they would begin all over again.

Hugh forced himself to listen, and he was struck by the irony of her saying that she had not seen him in church. She would not have seen him there even if he had lived in Los Angeles. Father Hugh was not a church priest. He was a university professor, someone who wrote articles and essays. He wasn't a minister who married people and baptized their babies. He was a scholar who published works that other researchers read. He was this, and more, because he had also become part of his university's inner core, the handful of men who ran the institution. He had always taken pride in his work, and he hadn't missed what he presumed was the dreary life of a priest attached to a church or to a pulpit or to a confessional. On the contrary, he had enjoyed being a scholar; and he had loved the excitement of power even more.

"What the Hell am I doing here?"

The priest was mumbling, thinking that he must have looked repulsive. Struggling to keep his glazed eyes open, he ran his fingers through his red hair, disheveled and gummy with the grime of the shelter. He felt his jaw prickling with more than a day's growth. He thought of the killing that was going on out on the streets.

"Hughie, boy, you're part of the package. How do you think they got those weapons?"

The voice rang unexpectedly in the priest's head, physically jolting him. His surprise was momentary, however. Father Hugh had grown used to the twanging noise that had robbed him of sleep night after night ever since Augie Sinclaire had died in a plane crash. The priest hated the voice. As always, he wanted to drown it out.

"Shut up! "

"What did you say, Padre? You want me to be quiet?"

"No, Señora. *Por favor,* I was thinking of something else. I'm listening to you."

"I arrived here a few days ago; I was thrown out of Los Angeles ..."

The woman abruptly interrupted what she was saying, then looked at the priest, "Tell me, Padre, what's your name?"

"Me llamo Padre Hugo."

He was surprised that he had used the Spanish version of his name. He repeated, "Sí, me llamo Hugo."

"Padrecito Hugo, why did you leave your land where you were safe? Why did you come here to where there's only death and sadness? When did you get here? Did others come with you?"

The woman's questions grated on the priest's nerves. He was feeling dizzy, and he began to sweat. He didn't know what to say, so he kept silent.

"What's the matter, Hughie? Scared of the old bag's questions? Go on,

tell her the truth."

Father Hugh ignored the voice reverberating in his head. Instead he tried to smile at the woman, but he gave up, knowing that he would look ridiculous, artificial. He was relieved to hear the roar of the helicopters and the machine guns tearing at the Salvadoran night since the noise blocked out the sarcastic voice ringing in his ears. The priest turned his attention to the woman.

"Padrecito, I'm frightened for myself, but especially for my son. He might be out there in the darkness hearing somebody's confession. He was preparing to be a priest, just like you. Or perhaps he's helping someone to die in peace. I'm going out to search for him."

The woman made an attempt to stand. It was difficult; her knees seemed too weak for her bulky body.

"No, no, Señora, sit down, please. You can't go right now. None of us can. We have to stay here until daylight, or until the fighting stops. Try to rest. Look at the others. They're all trying to regain some of their strength."

She looked around as the priest had asked her to do. "No, Padre," she said, "my son might be waiting for me. I'm his mother and I must look for him. I feel it here." She pointed at her heart. "I know in here that I'll find Bernabé."

"Wait for awhile. Why don't you stay and tell me about yourself and about your son? You say you've been in Los Angeles. Let's talk. Maybe, yes, yes, maybe I do know something of your son Bernardino."

"Bernabé. Not Bernardino."

The woman lumbered back to the cement floor where she sat and turned to the priest. "Padre, I need to confess,"she said softly.

Her face reflected an intensity that surprised Father Hugh. He didn't want to hear her confession. He had not heard one in years.

"Señora, I'm sorry to say that I'm not prepared."

"What do you mean, Padre? Isn't a priest always prepared for these things?"

"I mean I don't even have a stole or...."

"That means nothing to me. You're a priest, and that's all that matters!"

Father Hugh was angered by the woman's tone. He felt cornered, forced into doing what he didn't want to do. He remembered, however, that her silence meant the return of the carping voice.

"Very well, Señora. Begin."

"Padre, my name is Luz Delcano, and I'm a sinner. My son Bernabé is the love of my life, but he's the fruit of my sin. I loved his father, and I allowed him to love me even though he was married to another woman. I have never regretted nor repented of my love. That's a sin, isn't it?"

The priest was irritated by the woman's question.

"Loving is not a sin."

"I'm sorry, I didn't mean love. I know that's not a sin. I mean, not repenting! I've never repented of what I did. If Bernabé's father appeared here, right now, I would do everything with him all over again. Sometimes, at night especially, I think that when I die I'll go to Hell. But, we're already in Hell. What do you think, Padre Hugo?"

Luz's words were drifting away and the priest's mind began to wander. He was thinking of Hell, of repenting, and of being sorry for one's deeds.

"Bet you never felt sorry either, did you Hughie? Not you, big time priest that you always were. Who would have known you were such a son of a bitch?"

Hugh shut his eyes and ordered his brain to listen to the woman. He was suddenly glad to be hearing her confession because it blocked out the words echoing in his ears.

"Today, I went to my old barrio here in San Salvador near Santa Marta. I found my comadre Aurora crying because her husband had been killed. I can't imagine why anyone would kill him since he was a good man. He used to drink a little too much sometimes, but he was a good man."

Father Hugh knew that this was no longer a confession, but he didn't interrupt because he feared returning to his own thoughts. So he listened to Luz's rambling conversation.

"My comadre Aurora had three sons, but she told me that they've all disappeared. Now that her husband is dead who knows how she'll be able to live. Padrecito, my friend Aurora is practically a cripple. Many years ago, even before the death of our Archbishop, she was washing clothes by the river along with the rest of us. Suddenly we heard gunshots. All the other women ran, but Aurora wanted to gather her things, and she lost valuable time. When she finally did run, it was too late. A bullet shattered her knee. We dragged her to the hospital, but by the time her wound received attention, it was too late. Her leg couldn't be straightened. Now she walks like a spider, jerking her leg backward and forward in tiny steps, making her body go up and down. Pobrecita."

"Señora, I absolve you...."

"No, Padre, I'm not finished! I have more to tell you. Look at me, please. If you look at my face carefully you'll see many things right there. Por favor, mire. Look at my face. What do you see?"

Father Hugh strained in the gloom to look at Luz's face.

"I see a fine face."

"You're wrong! Forgive me, Padre, but your eyes do not see the truth. They don't see that on the inside of me is a lake of black, stinking mud, just like someone already in Hell!"

The priest was surprised by the intensity with which the woman spoke. She was speaking in English, and even though it lilted with a heavy accent, Luz's words conveyed her conviction. Father Hugh's words were a whisper.

"Forgive me, Señora, but I don't see any sin. I don't see mud."

"Do you know that I was almost shot when I wandered through the barrios? Do you know what I saw? I saw many people killed right in front of me. They were running in every direction trying to escape the bullets that were flying back and forth. Some of those poor people even waved white flags, not real flags, but rags and tablecloths, even shirts. They hoped that the killing might go somewhere else. But their flags didn't help them, because everywhere there were bodies, and parts of bodies. The stink of human shit was awful."

Luz became silent, again prompting Hugh to ask if she had finished her confession.

"No, Padre, I have more to say. I'm a sinner, and I ask you to bless me because I have sinned many times. When I was a child, just thirteen years old, I caused my grandfather to commit a grave sin. It was my fault. Of that I have always been certain, because you see, at the time he was old and past the time of temptation. I've been paying ever since then."

Luz began to sob; her crying was loud. One or two refugees stirred, making shussing sounds.

"Señora, God forgives us our transgressions. He knows our weaknesses, and He doesn't look for vengeance."

"No!"

Again the woman's intensity startled the priest. He regretted the platitudes.

"Some sins are unforgivable, Padre," she whispered hoarsely. "Like the sins of my people. Why do you think we're being killed like pigs? It's because of our sins, because we have done only what our bodies tell us to do, and we have never listened to what is good in this life."

"Señora, you're wrong! Those people out there are being slaughtered, not because of their sins but because of the greediness and cruelty of others."

She remained silent, waiting for the priest to continue, but instead he was giving in to the inner voice.

"Hugh, you're a god-damn hypocrite! Cut the crap, and stop pointing the finger at others. Go on! Tell her about your own greed. Why don't you 'fess up to your own sins? Tell the old bag that it's you who's the slime bucket, not her."

Father Hugh forced himself to stifle Augie's voice.

"Señora, please go on with your confession," he encouraged.

II

Luz Delcano finished her confession. The priest remained silent for several minutes before he spoke. "Señora," he told her gently, "that would not have been your fault. What happened was not your sin; it was your grandfather's."

She, too, was quiet before responding. Then she told him, "It's no use, Padre. Nothing will change. Besides, what's the difference. It's all in the past."

Luz fell into a deep silence while the distant sounds of barking dogs penetrated the walls of the shelter during a lull in the fighting. When the explosions started again, the howling stopped. The sudden blasts startled Father Hugh and his head jerked involuntarily, causing a sharp pain in his neck. He allowed his thoughts to wander vaguely, without direction.

Voices from the neighborhood where he grew up echoed faintly in his head, blocking out the reverberation of rifle and machine gun fire. Hugh was hearing distant sounds. They were so faint that his body tensed in an attempt to distinguish them. Suddenly his ear caught the lilting sounds of a boy's voice, that of a soprano singing in the parish choir. He recognized his voice. The Latin words sharpened, transporting the priest to Sunday Benediction.

"Tantum ergo Sacramentum Veneremur cernui..."

He then saw the image of the small house where he and his brothers and sister had grown up. He saw the stark, impoverished kitchen where his mother listlessly hunched over a rusty sink while his father, seated at the table, stared blankly at her.

The apparition seemed to cast a bright light in the shelter's darkness. The street where he ran and played ball with other boys and girls took shape in Father Hugh's head. Things were so vivid that he reached out, expecting to touch something in front of him.

"¿Qué pasa, Padre? Do you want something?"

"No, Señora. I'm trying to pray. Trate de dormir."

Father Hugh hoped the woman would do as he asked and try to sleep. He now wanted to be left alone with his thoughts, to give in to the exhaustions of the day's events. He was fatigued by the dreary plane trip and by the shock of finding San Salvador gripped in a battle that was bloodier and larger than he had imagined. Above all, he had not expected to be hustled into that bleak shelter filled with strangers, without knowing when it would be safe for him to leave.

The priest had left his university without the benefit of a leave of absence, so desperate was his need to escape the sleepless nights during which he was tormented by voices and faces from his past. Father Hugh had told himself that those disturbances were caused by his mind, which was tired and playing tricks on him. He was convinced that the stress of recent events in his life was taking its toll on his nerves, and he had been certain that if he gave himself a fresh start, his agitation would disappear.

The voices were again surfacing, however. It was as if his memories had sniffed out his trail, tracking and finding him among the terrified refugees in the shelter. Father Hugh, too weary to resist, surrendered to his gloomy thoughts, and the images out of his past glided in his direction, turning as he slumped against the concrete wall. There was Señor Costa, the neighborhood baker. His hands and arms were powdered white with flour. The dead man nodded, smiling his toothy smile at Hugh as he handed him one of his fruit turnovers. The priest noticed the sarcasm and mockery stamped on the dead man's face.

As the baker's image melted into the wall and disappeared from sight, Hugh thought he saw his mother walking toward him, gingerly stepping over the refugees' bodies. Her face was tired and drained of color, as it had been during her entire lifetime. Wordlessly, she stretched her thin arm toward Hugh, tenderly caressing his cheek and forehead. He felt the callouses on her palm and fingers.

"Say something, Ma. Just because you're dead doesn't mean you can't talk. Tell me why you let Pa work you into your grave?"

Immediately, his mother vanished into the air.

Father Hugh rubbed his eyes knowing that they were playing tricks on him, making him believe that he was dreaming while he was still awake. But the apparitions would not disappear. His sister Fiona, her long, red hair shining as it did when they played in the sun, approached Hugh and teased him with names that he knew were filled with the special affection she had for him, just because he was the youngest.

"Hey, Screwy Hughie! What's up Paddy Waddy?"

Why did she always call him Paddy Waddy? He wasn't even named Patrick. Hugh told himself that he would ask Fiona why she used that name. Then he remembered that his sister was dead. She had died several years before, giving birth to twins. He suddenly felt the full regret of never again asking Fiona anything or telling her that he had loved her almost as much as he loved his mother.

When Hugh looked again he sensed that the figure looking down at him was not his sister after all. It was Sister Philomena, his seventh grade teacher. Her wimple was very white and it glowed in the darkness of the shelter as if it were a saint's aura. Hugh remembered that she too was dead. Why were they all dead, he wondered. As if reading his thoughts, she sternly shook her head, as she had often done when he was a boy in her classroom.

"Mr. Joyce, stop staring at me as if I were a soul out of Purgatory. Now, you just get down to your lessons, and stop your day dreaming."

The round, soft vowels of her Irish brogue were ringing in Hugh's memory when suddenly they blurred with Father Cyprian's baritone voice.

"Hugh, we must all remember that in the end we'll be judged by how much we've loved during our lifetime. Love will be the only measure, not how successful we've been, and much less how powerful we become. Learn this well now that you're a novice."

Father Hugh looked up, convinced that he was seeing his novice master wagging his long index finger at him. He noticed that the old priest was not wearing trousers; he was clad only in his shorts. Even in death, Father Cyprian had forgotten to put on his pants, as had happened when his memory withered during his last years. Hugh wished that he could forget Father Cyprian's words as easily as the old man forgot his pants, but the image would not go away.

"Hugh, I see that you still think that being a good priest is a matter of following rules, up front where others can see. Well, you're wrong, you know. It is what's in here that counts."

Father Cyprian turned his long finger, pointing to his heart.

Hugh rubbed his eyes and shook his head hoping to get rid of the image. He regretted having asked Luz to keep quiet.

"¡Señora, despierte, por favor! Tell me more about yourself!"

Luz would not respond, so he was forced to go back to his memories. Father Cyprian was still standing in front of him, his stiff finger pointing at him accusingly, provoking a fresh surge of guilt in Hugh. He fought the feeling, reminding himself that he had always been a good priest; that he had always tried to be good.

Hugh began to see that an arm was looped around Father Cyprian's shoulders, and even though the gloom made it difficult to see him clearly, Hugh knew who it was. It was Father Virgil Canetti, and he was having difficulty keeping his arm around Father Cyprian's shoulders. Father Virgil had been a small man.

Hugh was not surprised at what he was experiencing because Cyprian and Virgil had recently made daily practice of interrupting his sleep. The visits had started to happen right after Father Virgil's death a few months back. The two priests always appeared in Hugh's dreams just before dawn, when the night dipped to its blackest pitch and, when together, they asked the same carping questions, pointing incriminating fingers that made Hugh break out with sweat.

The two black pools of Father Virgil's eyes persisted in looking at Hugh, forcing him to hunch over and bury his head between his bent knees. He remained in that position for several minutes.

"Hey, Pal, what's with the head stuck in the old crotch?"

Hearing Augie's voice, Hugh looked up. Father Cyprian and Father Virgil had vanished, and in their place stood Hugh's boyhood friend. He stared mockingly at Hugh, his smile cocky and self-confident as it had been when he was alive. The apparition held a half-smoked cigar in his right hand, while the other one tugged at his left leg, the artificial one.

A sudden blast of helicopter fire frightened everyone in the shelter. Father Hugh tried to focus his eyes in an effort to make out faces among those in the shelter, but it was useless. They were all faceless silhouettes. Hugh turned to look at Luz. He saw that she was awake, but lost in thought. The din had not disturbed her. When he returned to his own memories, he realized that Augie's shadow had evaporated into the thin, stale air.

III

Augustin Gerald Sinclaire had been the dreamer of the two boys. He constantly fantasized about himself and his future life. At times he was a pirate, born in another time, somewhere on an exotic island. Sometimes his fancy transformed him into an internationally known scientist, an explorer, even a discoverer. He saw himself traveling to unknown places.

During class, when Sister Philomena spoke of the Church's great evangelizers and martyrs, Augie day-dreamed seeing himself as a missionary, ready to surrender his life to cannibalistic savages. This dream had a twist though, for the savages would decide not to devour their victim after all. Instead, they would beg the humble missionary to become their archbishop, or more often their cardinal. Then the dream shifted, and he would find himself in other lands, not as a missionary but transformed into a monarch, or even an emperor.

If Augie was the dreamer, Hugh was the planner. Even when the boys were still in grammar school, Hugh would come up with schemes to counter Augie's dreams. Sister Philomena would reprimand Hugh for day-dreaming in class, when what he was really doing was planning. He was well aware of what life expected of him.

"Don't you want to grow up to be real rich, Hughie? I do."

"Nope. I'm going to be a priest."

"Aw, get out of here! Just because Sister said that those guys are big shots."

Hugh was convinced of what he wanted in life even then. He also knew what he did not want. He did not want his family's shabby life with its threadbare, gray existence. He did not want to be like his brothers who were content to work in factories and gas stations. Hugh did not want to be like his father who worked like a mule, and came home at day's end to eat in morose dejection, slowly killing his wife with silence and disdain.

"I hated you, Pa. Did you know that? I hated you for being poor, and because you didn't mind working until you dropped dead like a worn out nag. I couldn't stand you because of what you did to Ma. You treated her like dirt, and even though you saw that she was dying, you did nothing. Nothing!"

The priest saw his father's face looking at him in the darkness. His face wore the dull expression it always did when he looked at his son.

"Yeh, yeh, Pa. You thought I didn't know anything. Right? Well, you were wrong. You were the jerk, not me."

Hugh would be a priest, not just an ordinary one but an important member of the Church's priesthood. Sister Philomena told him, not once but many times, that a priest could become a bishop or even a cardinal of the Church. Even then he figured that if a young man could choose that way of life, why should he waste time on little aspirations. Why not aim at being a cardinal?

On the day they graduated from high school, Hugh told Augie of his intention to enter the novitiate by the end of that summer. The news took Augie by surprise. Even though he had known of his friend's plans ever since he could remember, he still felt shaken to think that Hugh would take the first step while he was still daydreaming. Before he knew what he was saying, Augie blurted out, "Hughie, I'm coming with you."

"You're crazy," Hugh said quickly, "What about your plans to become a millionaire? And what makes you think you can join up, just like that?" Hugh snapped his fingers as he nervously waved his right hand in the air.

"Look, Augie, first you've got to apply, then take a bunch of tests, and then, if you get that far, you've got to be interviewed, and then maybe, just maybe, you might be accepted. Just remember, Augie, you don't have a vocation."

"That's a crock, and you know it! Vocation, schmocation. What's that have to do with anything? Come on, Hughie, admit it! You're going into it for the same reasons everybody else does, so don't try to pull that vocation crap on me!"

Hugh felt a strange sensation. He wanted to hit Augie for implying that he was a hypocrite or an opportunist. He was offended that his closest friend could suggest that he aspired to the priesthood for anything less than reasons of dedication. His irritation, however, was caused by something deeper than insult. He felt an inexplicable emotion, as if Augie had inadvertently touched a secret niche in his heart, pressing it with the tip of his finger.

Turning his face away from his friend, Hugh told himself that he did have a vocation to the priesthood, that he had been called by God. He repeated this several times, trying to convince himself. He thought that the shaky feeling prompted by Augie's words was nothing less than a temptation against his calling, and he would not allow himself to give in to it. Hugh turned to Augie.

"Aw, shoot! What do I know, Augie. If you want to come along, who am I to say anything? But you'd better get the ball rolling if you really want to be part of the group entering this Fall. Go ahead, try it and see, but if I were you I wouldn't bet my bottom dollar on being accepted."

"You make it sound as if I was about to sign up for the next train to Heaven, Hughie old man. It's just another summer camp as far as I'm concerned. You just watch your old pal. Come on! What's with the big horse face? You really didn't think you could get rid of me that easy, did you?"

Hugh's annoyance with his friend increased with each word. He knew that Augie would be accepted to the novitiate because he had that kind of luck. He felt cheated because he wanted to walk alone down his life's path without anyone tagging along or depending on him. Now his resolve to be alone among the best was diminishing.

Hugh had been right. Augie was accepted into the novitiate that Fall of 1957. Certain exceptions had been made. A few short cuts were taken in the process because, as the final report stated, Augustin Sinclaire demonstrated notable piety and other worthy talents.

In September, the Joyces and Sinclaires rambled to the entrance of the novitiate. The grounds, covered with grape vines, were a blur of golds and reds and yellows, and the air, which sometimes was oppressively hot during that time of the year, was crisp and transparent. Showing the confidence he was feeling, Augie entered the novitiate's wide front door strutting as if he were a hero. He grinned broadly at his boyhood friend, then whispered, "I guess it'll be more fun yanking on it in here than out there, eh, Hughie?"

Hugh pretended not to have heard. He wished that Augie had been struck dead for speaking as he had in that sacred place. He was disgusted with Augie's vulgarity and coarseness, and he wished with all his heart that Augie had been rejected. Above all Hugh desired to put his impoverished life behind him, to begin a new life with different friends and ideas. This would now be impossible with

Augie pulling at his sleeve.

Augie, however, was not cut out for the priesthood. The rigors of novitiate life soon began to rub like sandpaper against his flesh. What in the beginning had been fun, soon became torture for him. The long hours of silence, interrupted only by the study of courses in Latin, Greek, philosophy and theology ate at Augie's nerves like termites. He was intelligent, but his disposition pulled him away from anything abstract. He hated the books he was assigned to read, and he detested his teachers even more.

"Who in the Hell cares what the Hyper... the Hyper... the Hypersthenic Union is? You tell me, Hugh. Who gives a shit?"

"You mean Hypostatic Union."

"You see? I can't even pronounce the stupid word."

The discipline of novitiate life wore at Augie's spirit, often reducing him to tears. He felt humiliated when this happened, and he tried to keep it to himself, but inevitably, during the brief moments in which the novices were allowed to speak, Augie's conversations were filled with complaining and belly-aching. The daily routine fatigued him, and he was especially restless in chapel during the long periods set aside for prayer, when he felt bored and resentful. Whenever he looked at his fellow novices, he became frustrated and irritated because they seemed lost in a trance that he found unexplainable.

Augie detested the Novice Master. He called him Old Fart behind his back, or Gasher or Bulldog because of the priest's prominent lower jaw. Most of all, Augie hated the cassock the novices were obligated to wear at all times, and he resented that he was forbidden to remove it during the day even when working in the garden or doing other types of work. Augie cheated on this rule, as he did with all the others rules, especially the one that demanded that the novices observe silence.

He was especially depressed by the Grand Silence, the period that began with late evening, dragging on through the night, and into the morning hours until after breakfast. It was at those times that the novices seemed like robots to Augie, unthinking idiots who obeyed without speaking or asking questions, and he hated all of them because of their docility.

Hugh, unlike Augie, gave himself wholeheartedly to the life expected of a novice. When the bell to rise sounded in the early morning, he sprang out of bed, offering its difficulty as a sacrifice for the forgiveness of sin and for the Holy Souls in Purgatory. He mouthed his prayers with as much fervor as possible, and he gave all of his energy to the assigned work and studies. He even told himself that he enjoyed speaking Latin at table during meals, an exercise hated by the rest of the novices. Hugh, who excelled in the language, unabashedly showed off. He didn't know it, but his fellow novices competed with one another just to sit at the same table with him. Since he did all the talking, it relieved them of having to struggle through the intricate Latin conjugations.

He was successful in every aspect of his novitiate formation, even where chastity was concerned. Whenever he overheard other novices speaking of their recurring temptations and sexual urges, Hugh felt relieved because he was free of that struggle. Even when the novice master asked him about his feelings and impulses, Hugh claimed that he did not experience any difficulty.

At night, however, during the hours when his mind and will fell into deep sleep, Hugh lost control over his thoughts. It was then that he was unable to wrestle with vivid images of men and women engaging in sexual intercourse. Even though he denied it during his waking moments, Hugh frequently woke up at night thinking he heard groaning and sighing and the squeaking of a bed. Whenever this happened, it did not take Hugh long to realize that it had been he who had been moaning, he who was aroused and wet. At daybreak, however, when he regained control of his mind and sensations, Hugh suppressed this detested and embarrassing experience by denying it to himself, making certain never to think about what happened to him almost nightly.

Hugh had other secrets as well. He never told anyone of the silvery voice of ambition to which he listened carefully since his first days as a novice all the way through his years as a priest. Calling it dedication, Hugh surrendered to his need for prestige, for recognition, refusing to be satisfied with anything less than being in first place at all times and in all things. It was his secret as well that he disdained any weakness in his brother priests, that he looked down on any priest who blundered or fell into sin. The other side of his contempt for weakness was that Hugh judged power and control to be greater than mercy and humility. In his mind, only those priests in places of authority and influence were good priests.

As Hugh molded himself to fit his own image of the priesthood, Christmas of 1957 neared, and Augie was finally forced to admit to his friend that he was not made for that life. He said little to Hugh when he left the novitiate early one morning, only a few words about keeping in touch. Hugh was unmoved; he felt nothing except relief. He convinced himself that God had manifested His will, at last relieving him of Augie's crudeness and vulgarity.

It was a different story for Augie, however. He felt strange leaving his friend for the first time since they had been boys. He wanted to tell Hugh that surely he would one day be a great and important priest, probably a bishop, maybe even a cardinal. Augie wanted to tell his friend what he had never before told him. He wanted Hugh to know that he admired him, that he would miss him, and that he could always depend on him for anything. His friend's aloofness, however, discouraged Augie from saying anything.

When Augie walked away from the novitiate on a rainy December morning, he had no purpose, he didn't even know where to go. So he drifted. He made his way on freight trains that crisscrossed small, dingy towns that promised little and inspired him less. He hitched truck rides down endless stretches of highway that unraveled like black ribbons over baked desert ground. He spent days and nights with transients and hobos with whom he found comfort in a shared pint of cheap whiskey and rough talk. Augie was not unhappy in that world; he even liked it. He could be himself, use the vulgar language with which he best expressed himself, and laugh his rough, loud guffaws without faces turning in his direction, without eyebrows lifting.

A few months of aimless wandering, however, were enough. He settled in Las Vegas, where he was able to get a job dealing blackjack at night and filling in as a part-time hotel doorman during the day. Since he was quick with his hands and even faster with his talk, Augie found fast, easy success in that city. He became a sharp dresser wearing pin-striped suits and wing-tip shoes, and he always had a wad of bills bulging in his pocket. Eventually he purchased a 1958 Cadillac Coupe de Ville on an installment plan. Through it all, Augie felt good with the crowd he was able to associate with, especially the women. He usually dealt the cards until his shift ended, then polished off the night in a motel with a woman whose name he frequently didn't know.

As the years passed Augie became a faster talker than most of his friends and learned how to run with the brightest and most important people in town. He made solid contacts with men who held big money and bigger ideas on how to get more of it. During it all he never forgot Hugh, mentioning his name whenever he was with buddies and girlfriends, usually when he was high on booze.

"Did I ever tell you guys about my old buddy Hugh Joyce? I have? Well, don't forget, he's a priest, or almost one. I bet none of you bums have a friend like mine."

Augie's boast was usually met with a here-we-go-again look from those listening but he remained unruffled. He was proud of Hugh in a way that would have embarrassed the young priest. During those years, Augie kept in touch with his friend, writing him letters that told little about his own life, and that were instead filled with questions regarding Hugh's life.

Hugh responded, gladly providing Augie with pages describing the stages of his formation as a novice. He wrote about his novitiate days, which came to an end when he pronounced vows of chastity, poverty and obedience. Some years later, Hugh explained in his letters that he was now assigned to study philosophy somewhere in Europe.

"You see what I mean, Babe? Here's this letter that tells how Hughie is studying this boring stuff, a real pain in the ass, believe me. No one can make sense out of the crap. And he does it full-time, non-stop! What'd I tell you? A real brain! And we grew up together, on the same stinking street. What do you say to that? Can you believe it? Well, don't just sit there staring at me. Say something! Aw, you're too dumb to know what I'm talking about."

The letters between the two men were consistent even though in time Augie began to experience mixed feelings regarding Hugh's responses. He sometimes felt envious of his friend, wishing that he had Hugh's clarity of purpose and his confidence. At these times, Augie comforted himself remembering that Hugh was not free like he was, and that he would always be obligated to obey someone or something. Most of all, Augie was glad that he was not in his friend's shoes, especially when it came to women. He told himself that he couldn't even begin to imagine a world without them. At other times, however, Augie could not help representing Hugh's bragging.

"I've written an essay that's about to appear in the next *Review.*"

These comments from Hugh dominated his letters to Augie, which frequently conveyed news of his work and his publications. Augie felt annoyed that his friend sang his own praises. At those times, however, he found reasons to ignore his exasperation.

"Oh, what the Hell! What else does the poor jerk have anyway?" The letters between Hugh and Augie continued for years. In 1967,

Augie received a letter telling of Hugh's approaching ordination, to be followed by his first mass a few days later. Augie, however, had already received the notice of his induction into the army. Three months later, on the day in which Hugh's hands were anointed by the bishop, Augie's leg was ripped from his body by a Vietcong mine. Days later, Hugh celebrated his first Mass. While he whispered the sacred words of the Consecration, Augie, in anguish and pain, blasphemed God, and cursed Christ's mother and all the saints in Heaven. While Hugh, radiant and surrounded by proud friends and relatives, accepted congratulations and admiring smiles, Augie, lost in a morphine-induced nightmare, was hallucinating and screaming out Hugh's name.

Unknown to Father Hugh, by the time he delivered his first university lecture, Augie was a different man. Not only was he missing a part of his body but the carnage with which he had lived had blocked out his awe for his old friend. Augie was a changed man by then. He wept tears of rage and frustration knowing he would end his days as a cripple. He understood with bitterness that, even though he was only twenty seven years old, he had no other prospect but to depend upon the kindness of others.

IV

"Padrecito, are you asleep? I need to speak some more. But... maybe you need to sleep...I'm sorry."

Father Hugh was not sleeping. He was lost in the gloom of his memories, and his eyes shut tight against the sentiments he was experiencing. The night seemed eternal to him, refusing to end. Outside, on the streets of San Salvador, the blasting and explosions went on without interruption. Luz spoke rapidly, rambling from one word to another in a shaky attempt to gather her ideas.

"I'm a Delcano. Do you know what that means Padre Hugo? It means that I should be over there in Escalón, safe and secure with the rich people. It means that my sons should be with me, that we should all be sheltered and not lost in this world. I should not be here in this rat hole."

Father Hugh felt uneasy wit Luz's words because he was unable to decipher their meaning. She didn't look as if she were a member of the Salvadoran wealthy or of a family such as the Delcanos. He had done business with a Colonel Delcano, but Hugh felt certain that it couldn't have been the same family.

Luz seemed to know his thoughts.

"Padre, you're criticizing me, aren't you? I know that you don't believe what I'm saying, but I have reason to speak this way. I'm a member of a very wealthy family. Now, you're staring at me as if I were crazy! ¡Una loca! I just told you in my confession that my grandfather was Lucio Delcano, and that he was very rich, very powerful. I'm part of that family. Is it my fault that he never married my grandmother? Is it my fault that I was forced off the Delcano land as soon as the old grandfather died?"

Father Hugh's attention latched on to what the woman was saying about the family name and about her sons.

"Sons? Did you say sons, Señora? I thought you had only one

son. Bernabé."

"Sí. I said sons."

She emphasized her last word, and to make sure that the priest understood, Luz repeated it several times. "¡Hijos, hijos, hijos! I had a son before Bernabé. He was a child that I had from what I told you I did with my grandfather. You're surprised, I see. Well, it's true. My son was born some months after my grandfather died. The old man died without knowing that I was going to have his baby. "

Luz 's words came to her with difficulty, and she spoke in short, terse phrases. "But the rest of his family knew," she said. "They were afraid of what my son might become if he remained with those of us who were poor. So the boy was taken away from me. I've never seen him since the day Damián Delcano came to our hut. He was one of the old grandfather's sons, and also the one who stole my son. I was just a girl myself, but don't think that it was easy for him. No, Señor, no fue fácil para él. I ran after him as he walked away with my baby in his arms. I screamed and pulled at Damián's sleeves. I was even able to scratch at his face, and once I bit him on his hand. I begged but he did it anyway."

Luz stopped talking. Her chest heaved up and down. When she spoke again, she whispered, "My son must be your age. How old are you?"

"I'm forty-six."

"Almost the same. He's forty-seven, this year."

Father Hugh's interest grew as the woman spoke. "Are you certain that he's alive?" he questioned. "What do you know of him?"

"Well, I know the name the family gave him when he was baptized, nothing else. Someone told me that the little boy had been named after Don Lucio, his father. I know also that my son is now a powerful man.

"Powerful? What do you mean?"

"He's in the military, Padre Hugo."

Father Hugh closed his eyes for a moment. The figure of the tall, slender man dressed in the uniform of a Salvadoran colonel appeared. His face was very white, his hair blond, and his eyes were blue. As he sat at his desk he held his hands in front of him, fingertips pressed together, like an angel in prayer.

"Well, what do you know, Hughie? What a small world! That's the son of a bitch colonel who did business with you all those times you came down here to peddle our hardware. His name was Lucio Delcano. Everyone called

him el Angel. Remember?"

Father Hugh silenced the whining voice.

"Señora, do you know what he looks like now?" he asked.

"¡Seguro que no! How could I know? That kind of person is up there, you know, in the clouds. People like me don't mix with his kind." She pointed her finger straight up. "But, I can tell you what he looked like when he was born. He was all Delcano. White, very white, and his eyes were blue. Can you believe me? Maybe not, because you're looking at me and all you see is my brown face. You don't have to believe me if you don't want to, but it's the truth."

The helicopters whirled overhead searching for the guerrillas who were escalating their attacks on the government forces. A blast from a missile made the shelter tremble, causing a flurry among those hiding inside. Luz, oblivious to what was happening outside, looked at the priest. Although it was dark, he could see her intense gaze.

He kept quiet as his breath came in short spurts. Even though he didn't want to know more about the woman, he didn't want to hear Augie's sarcastic voice either.

"Do you want to rest, Padre?"

"No. Not now. Tell me more about yourself. What about your mother and father? Where were they when all of this was happening to you?"

The woman sighed. After a while, she said softly, "I was alone when these things were happening. You see, I've been alone since I was a very little girl, and I've forgotten most things. I remember only that my father worked when the coffee beans were ready for harvesting, and that he traveled to different plantations where he stayed for months. I remember also that he used to come and go, and that one day he didn't return. I think that it wasn't too long afterwards that my mother became very sick, I don't know of what, I just know that she died. That left me with only one brother. He looked after himself and me."

"Señora, didn't he help you when he realized what your grandfather had done?"

"No. No. He felt ashamed of me. After Damián took my baby away, my brother forced me out of the hut where we lived, and because I didn't have anywhere else to go to, I came here to San Salvador. I never returned, so I have never seen my brother again. But I was happy to have come here because no one knew me or what I had done with the old man."

"Why do you call yourself a Delcano? Do you think others consider you part of that family? What I mean is...."

Luz was amused, and she teased the priest, almost forcing him to end his thought.

"Well, Padrecito?" Her face relaxed, and she smiled. When he didn't respond, she continued, "If you stop to consider, Padre, I know that you'll agree that no matter what anybody says, I am twice a Delcano. First, I'm a granddaughter of old Don Lucio and second, I'm his wife."

She paused for a moment, then added, "Padre, what do you think I am to Lucio my son? I know that I'm his mother. But am I also his great-grandmother, or maybe his sister? And what about me? What do you think I am to myself? Maybe I'm my own grandmother."

The priest could not be sure of what he thought he was seeing. Luz was resting her head against the wall, and her face was shrouded in shadows, but he felt that the woman was giggling quietly. Suddenly he felt depressed and sick. He thought she was lying to him, and laughing at him.

Luz became serious again. "When I came to San Salvador I was barely fourteen but I knew how to clean a house and how to wash clothes, so I found work and shelter in one of the grand homes over there." Luz's round chin pointed in the direction of the wealthy Escalón district.

"I liked it there from the beginning, and even though I was nothing but a homeless girl, the lady of the house was good to me. It's true, Padre. There's good and bad everywhere. Doña Blanca—that was her name—was a wealthy woman, one of the Grijalva family. She was beautiful, and she could have been arrogant and proud. But she wasn't. I remember her clearly. She was older than I was, but not too much older. I suppose she must have been twenty-five or so when I first began to work for her. She had two young daughters, and one of my obligations was to play with them when they weren't in school.

"Doña Blanca's husband was a lawyer and an important man who worked for the government. He, too, was not old. When he found out that I didn't know how to read or write, he told his wife that he would teach me, even though they knew that to teach someone like me to read was not approved of by most people of their station."

"How long were you with the Grijalva family?"

"Many years. I told you that when I began working with them I was fourteen years old, and when I left, I was thirty-one. During those years I learned to read and write, and how to speak, just as you now hear me. As I grew older, Doña Blanca placed more trust in me, and she made me the head of all the servants, both men and women. I was very happy.

"But there's something in me, Padre," Luz 's voice became a hoarse whisper, "there's a devil in me that makes me do bad things. Just like a cat that waits for a bird in silence, without the slightest motion, that's the way the shadow waits for me. I don't know when it will jump on me but it does."

The priest turned and gazed into the woman's eyes. In the gloom, they looked flinty black.

"During the first years, Doña Blanca's husband and I met for an hour every day for my lessons. I learned rapidly, and he seemed pleased. But after several years, when we no longer met for lessons, we began to do other things. Do you understand me, Padre?"

Wondering why Luz had not mentioned this part of her life during her confession, the priest blurted out, "Yes, I understand, and you need not continue. Perhaps you'd like to rest."

"But I must tell you now that I've begun. I was no longer a little girl. In fact, I was considered old. I was past my youth, and I was considered a *vieja quedada*. Do you remember what that means, Padre? In your language it means a woman who's lost her chance of marrying. It means...how do you say....an Old Bag.

"I admit that I longed for his visits to my room when we'd go to my bed, and there do it...things...you know what I mean...many times over. Even though I cared for Doña Blanca, still that cat that I was telling you about, the shadow that makes me do things, was more powerful.

"The day came when Doña Blanca began to suspect. One day she walked to the door of my room, opened it and saw her husband in bed with me. She remained calm. She neither shouted nor cried, as anyone would expect. She only closed the door and walked away. But I knew that I had to leave her house, and I did. I took only my clothes, and Bernabé, who by that time was in my belly."

Father Hugh kept quiet.

"Padrecito, you're angry with me, I can tell. Please forgive me for speaking of these things. Would you prefer to hear what happened to me after I lost Bernabé in front of the Cathedral?"

Hugh realized that Luz was expecting the admonitions a priest should give a woman in her situation, but he was fatigued and uncertain. He couldn't formulate the platitudes that usually were on the tip of his tongue. He didn't care if she had fornicated, then had no shame about it. Unable to say what he felt, he asked, "How did you make a living after you left the Grijalvas?"

"Not the way you're thinking, Padre Hugo!"

Luz 's head snapped in the priest's direction as she turned to look into his eyes. Her voice was dry as she said, "I left this city and went north. I got as far as a little town on the border, a small place called Carasucia. Ah, I see by your smile that you know what it means."

"Dirty Face? Is that what the town is called?"

Hugh wondered about the woman's strange sense of humor.

"*Sí*. Carasucia. There I decided to begin a new life cleaning houses and washing clothes. After some time I put up a small *puesto*—I don't know how to say that word in English—where I made a good living selling fruit and food."

Luz demonstrated her selling style to the priest. She opened her mouth, forming a black rectangle that framed her quivering tongue. "¡Pupusaaaaas! Melonesss...Sandíaaaas....Pepinoooos!"

Several voices shot out of the darkness telling her to keep quiet, that there were children trying to sleep, that the bombs were enough noise. She continued, oblivious to the shushing.

"For years I was able to make a living for me and my boy by working on street corners, and in the houses of Carasucia. I worked every day so that Bernabé could have a good education. I taught him what I knew of writing, and how to make his letters and I did this for him before he went to school. Bernabé was...is...very intelligent.

"When he was about fourteen years old, I decided that it would be better for him if we returned to the capital. You understand, the schools are better here, and he would be able to do something with his life. So we came. A woman like me, Padrecito, makes a life one way or another. Anyway, Escalón is there, and the rich ladies that live in those beautiful houses need someone to clean and wash their dirty underwear. I packed our few things, and returned to this city. That's when Bernabé and I moved into Barrio Santa Marta.

"But soon Bernabé began to ask me about his father, about where he came from. He wanted to know where he was born. I told him very little, Padre Hugo, and what I did tell him were mostly lies. I admit it. I didn't want him to know the truth about what I did with his father. I don't know why I kept this a secret. Do you think it was a mistake?"

Luz turned to Father Hugh. He was holding his knees in his arms, rocking back and forth.

"Padre, does your stomach hurt?" she asked.

"No!"

She was silent for a long time while the priest grappled with increasing crankiness. Her prattle was getting on his nerves.

"Did you ever tell Bernabé about your other son?" Hugh questioned.

"No!" Luz snapped out the word. "Why would I have told him? What good...?"

"It would have been better than all the lies, that's for sure! Maybe some good might have come from it, Señora. Did it ever occur to you that the two brothers might one day meet? Also, you've given Bernabé the Delcano name. Maybe that was a mistake. Maybe, just maybe, the family might find out and resent that you've taken that name. I mean...this place is small. Everyone seems to know one another."

Luz felt a rush of anger.

"Maybe, maybe! What do you know of these things? You know nothing! Nothing! I gave my son the only name he deserved. The name he received from the blood that fills his veins!"

Frustrated with the priest's questions, Luz mumbled under her breath, "¿Éste qué sabe? ¡Pendejo!"

Hugh heard the mumbling and understood her words. He resented the insult but sensed that both of them were on the verge of an argument. He murmured softly, "I do know, Señora. Believe me, I do."

V

Colonel Delcano's face, as Father Hugh remembered it from the last time he had negotiated with him, appeared in the darkness of the shelter. The priest saw it clearly; it seemed carved in white stone. Suddenly, the image distorted. It wrapped itself around Hugh's throat making him choke on saliva.

"What's the matter, Pal? You getting the heebbie-jeebies?"

Augie's voice sounded in the recesses of the priest's mind, shoving away the Colonel's face. Hugh looked around hoping that someone might interrupt but he saw only dark silhouettes of sleeping or huddling people. There was no one to relieve him of the memory of Augie, not even Luz, who was now angry and refusing to speak.

"Tell you what, Hughie Boy. What do you say we pray together? Remember Sister Philomena's prayers? She really was big on the litanies. You know, the ones that used to put all the kids to snoring. Come on! All you have to do is lead, and I'll answer."

Hugh closed his eyes. As if in a trance, the priest began to mumble, then to chant the prayers.

"Lord, have mercy..."

"Aw, come on, Hughie! Cut the preliminaries, and get to the meat and bones of the thing."

Father Hugh complied, then continued with the litany, "Seat of Wisdom..."

"You mean Seat of Caginess, don't you Pal?"

Hugh ignored the sarcasm. "Tower of Ivory...", he persisted.

"Ha! There you go again. How about Tower of Gold?"

Hugh began to sweat. He hated Augie's cynicism.

"Well, come on, get a move on it! Me and Sister are waiting for you, old Buddy. Go on with the prayers. Don't tell me that you've forgotten how to pray. You were always great at mouthing things, you know."

"Queen of the Apostles..."

"Got it all wrong again. You mean king, don't you Hughie? King of hypocrites, or maybe emperor of liars. You ought to know, because that's you, isn't it?

"Fuck you, Augie!"

The voice fell silent and Hugh was relieved. Suddenly, however, he thought he sensed Augie's presence; it moved closer each moment. He thought he heard a grunt as Augie plopped down next to him, leaning against the sticky wall. The priest thought he saw Augie stretch his artificial leg rigidly forward, then rub it with his hand.

"What's with the old bag? What's she staring at? Hasn't she ever seen a gimp before? "

Hugh looked to his side and saw that Luz was looking at him and not at Augie.

"¿Qué pasa, Señora? Aren't you able to sleep?"

"Padre, I thought I heard you praying, and I thought I would join you. But then you said strange things that I've never heard before."

"I must be falling asleep. Perdón, Señora."

Father Hugh stiffly turned his head to where Augie's shadow had been, hoping that it had disappeared. It was definitely there.

"You sure can whip out the Spanish, can't you? Not that I'm knocking it, Hughie. I admit it came in handy back when we were down here making our deals with these bastards. Remember? Sure you do. I can tell because you're sweating again."

Father Hugh remained silent. His eyes were shut, and his arms were folded over his chest.

"You know, Hugh, you really gall me. Look at you. You look like the picture of innocence with your eyes shut and head hanging low, just as if you were really feeling sorry."

"I *am* feeling sorry! I regret everything! That's what you want to hear, isn't it?"

"Feeling sorry! Ha! That's a laugh. As if I didn't know you, Chum. Who are you feeling sorry for? Yourself, right? Sure! I know because you've never given a damn about anyone except yourself. Let me tell you something about feeling sorry. Feeling sorry is when you're laying on a stretcher, waiting your turn to be hauled onto a growling chopper because your leg has been blown to hell and back. Sorry is laying flat on your belly in a stinking hospital bed, crying your eyes out, just like a baby, while a nurse is wiping your ass because you're too useless to do it for yourself. Sorry is knowing that you're going to be nothing but a bum for the rest of your life because, Baby, all you've got is a plastic leg to stand on, and three hundred

lousy bucks in your pocket. Let me tell you, Kid, sorry is seeing other human beings blown to bits right in front of your eyes. Sorry is ..."

"Shut up, Augie. Just shut up, will you? Now, who's being the phony! You make me sick to my stomach. I could puke right on top of you! You talk of people being blown up. Now, you tell me, just how do you think you became a millionaire, huh? Come on, speak up. I'm fed up with these little games you play on me every night. If I'm a liar and a hypocrite, so are you! You're the one that snagged me into..."

"Into what, Pal? Into giving you exactly what you wanted from that stinking university? Into making you the center of attention? Look, what you and I did was business, pure business, and if a few people got killed somewhere along the line...well, tough!"

Hugh thought of how it had all started, and of how simple it had been. Simple and deadly. His and Augie's renewed association began with a letter addressed to the president of the university and written on Augustin Sinclaire Enterprises stationery. Along with the letter, a check in the amount of one million dollars had been enclosed. The message was brief. The money was an unconditional donation to be used to assist needy students. The letter was signed with Mr. Augustin Sinclaire's tight, small signature, and followed by a post-script that casually sent best regards to his friend, Father Hugh Joyce.

That same evening before dinner, Father President had approached Hugh to tell him of Mr. Sinclaire's donation and of his personal greeting. When the president asked him why he had kept his friendship a secret, Hugh replied that he had not heard from Sin-claire in a number of years.

In fact, Hugh was stunned by the news of the donation because he had not imagined that Augie had really become the millionaire of his boyhood dreams. Hugh was also surprised because he had not heard from him in years. The last time they had met had been after Augie's return from the war when he had unexpectedly visited Hugh at the university. The priest remembered that he had been embarrassed by the shabby man who approached him in front of his campus colleagues. Hugh had felt disgusted by Augie's uncombed long hair and beard, and he had not known how to react when he saw him hobbling awkwardly on a cane. Instead of sympathy, Hugh had felt repugnance when Augie good naturedly attempted to embrace him. Even now, after all those years, Hugh could still smell the rancid odor of tobacco and alcohol that had clung to Augie. That stench, he recalled, had nauseated him.

After that first encounter, Augie tried several times to reach Hugh by phone, but the priest refused to answer his calls. He was ashamed of the man who had been his boyhood friend. When a few more attempts to contact Hugh failed, Augie gave up. He took time only to scribble Hugh a note promising never to forget that he had rejected him.

Father Hugh now chose to block out that incident because things had evidently changed. His friend was wealthy, and since he had specifically asked the president to pass on his greetings to his old buddy, Hugh assumed that Augie must have forgotten their last meeting. Besides, he was delighted to be the center of the president's attention and that of his fellow priests. There were toasts to him during the meal, and he was congratulated for having attracted a significant donation to the university.

Father Hugh was thrilled. He had been on the faculty for thirteen years, and even though he was recognized as a scholar and teacher by his department and the rest of his fellow professors, he had nonetheless felt left out of the core that governed the university. Unexpectedly, he now was being singled out and recognized. He was certain of this when the president invited him to sit at his table for dinner that night. He wanted, he said, to get acquainted with this old friend of Father Hugh's. Mr. Sinclaire seemed to be the type of supporter the university needed, the president emphasized, and what could be better than to have Hugh invite him to campus as soon as possible.

Father Hugh obliged the request.

"Took the bite, hook, line and sinker, didn't you Hughie? Just the way I knew you would. Nothing like money to make even a gimp like me look attractive. Man, oh man! Did you answer that letter of mine fast! Not like before when you wouldn't answer my phone calls after you found out that I was lame, when I needed you most. You should've come to visit me when I was down and out, when I was a bum, peddling pipes in that two bit hardware store. You were too much of a star, weren't you? But after all those years...ha!...that old moola, that mucho dinero, stopped you right in your tracks."

The priest held his head in his hands. Augie's voice whined in his ears, its tight accent crushing the words until they became almost incomprehensible. He thought of the years during which he had been a professor, and of how, after Augie's contributions, he was appointed to the Board of Trustees and, within a short while, he was made Executive Assistant to the president. Hugh had known then that the positions were due only to Augie's continued donations but he had accepted the assignments gladly and without question.

As the Sinclaire money continued to come in, Hugh gained prestige. Eventually he was even appointed chairman of the Finance Committee of the Board of Trustees. This last appointment caused dissention among several of the university administrators and faculty since Father Hugh's field of experience was not finance. The president ignored the opposition, however, and Hugh continued in that position.

Under Hugh Joyce's leadership, the Finance Committee proposed that the university invest large amounts of its funds in Augustin Sinclaire Enterprises, and the Board unanimously approved the plan. For every million dollars that Augie donated to the university, his firm received institutional monies in return to be invested in his business. These transactions went on for nearly ten years, even though only a cursory study had been made by the university of Augustin Sinclaire Enterprises and of how it generated its income and assets.

"Pipes. That was my business. Hardware and pipes."

"Contraband, you mean. Gun-running."

"But you knew it all the time and still lapped it up, Hughie old chum."

Unlike the Board of Trustees and the president of the university, Father Hugh knew how Augie had made his millions because his friend had told him everything down to the last detail. He realized that the Sinclaire business had initially been legitimate, and that his friend had started with nothing or practically nothing when he was discharged from the army. He was aware that Augie had arrived in Southern California when real estate and new construction were on the verge of unprecedented growth and development. Orange, Riverside and San Bernardino Counties had embarked on building projects involving tracts of private and mobile homes, condominiums and shopping malls, and Augie had been there with his fledgling hardware enterprise Father Hugh often thought of this, and of how Augie had come out of nothing, not only surviving but overcoming his physical disability.

The business of pipes and other related products made Augie successful and wealthy. The priest knew, however, that this wealth was underpinned by the even more lucrative business of buying contraband arms from undisclosed sources and selling them to the highest bidders. Only a handful of men, among them Father Hugh Joyce, knew that Augie had stayed in touch with former war buddies, and that through them he had established ties with unnamed, powerful sources who were willing to illegally peddle arms to any group.

"Pipes are chicken feed, Hugh, just peanuts. But a good cover, eh? Did anyone ever imagine where the real money came from? Sure, they did! They just didn't want to 'fess up to it.

Initially, Augie dealt with clients in the Middle East, but soon he calculated that compared to what was unfolding in Latin America, his Middle Eastern possibilities were limited. He switched his geographical focus, concentrating his attention on Central America. Augie dealt with a wide assortment of customers in different countries in that region. The identity of his buyers was unknown to most people, but Augie, through direct contact with them, knew that they were ministers and commissioners and colonels. He also knew that if he didn't do the selling to them, someone else would beat him to it. He concluded that he might as well be there first.

The business was tricky and dangerous, and it posed serious problems, the greatest being the need for secrecy. Transportation and delivery of cargos posed grave dangers. However, Augie's shrewdness, coupled with his gift for making new contacts and friends, made it possible for him to bypass the many hurdles of the business.

He developed a simple plan. Arms brokers secretly sold their goods to Augie at a lower than official price. He then peddled them to foreign military enclaves at inflated prices. The brokers were glad to unload their goods at a low price because Augie provided a solid, continuous market, and the foreign customers were equally open to him because he offered a lower than official price. It was of little importance to anyone that he walked away from the deal with his initial investment doubled.

Augie wanted more than two times what he invested though, so he set his sights on even bigger money. To achieve his goal, however, he knew that he needed additional capital. It was at this juncture that Augie Sinclaire and his money resurfaced in Hugh Joyce's life.

VI

"Money makes money, right Hughie? Give a little, take a little, that's the name of the game. Use the right bait, and those snappers will snap."

Augie's presence dominated the shelter, and his voice pounded stubbornly in Father Hugh's head. He wanted to squeeze it out of his hearing by pressing his hands against his skull, but Augie's jeering persisted, taunting the priest.

Hugh Joyce had been the snapper, and the bait had been the money that gave him the influence he had craved. When Augie had put his cards on the table, frankly revealing everything, Father Hugh had agreed to collaborate with no questions asked. Even though he recognized the implications of Augie's work, Hugh could not resist the wave of prestige on which it had placed him.

In 1979, one year after the guerrillas in El Salvador had made their first move, the undercover side of Augustin Sinclaire Enterprises, based mainly on university investments, was ready to do business on a wider scale. The company began with the guerrillas, but these clients were lured away and taken over by competitors from behind the Iron Curtain. Augie then switched his targeted market, turning to the government military enclave to barter his weaponry.

He invited Father Hugh to join him on several trips to the capital where they made contact with a man influential beyond even Augie's expectations. Colonel Lucio Delcano, attached to Army Intelligence, initially listened intently to their plans and offers. Their main selling point was that they, *los gringos* as Augie and Hugh became known, offered a way of undercutting prices quoted by other arms brokers. The lower prices offered by the Americans ultimately convinced Colonel Delcano. He, and the interests he represented, accepted to do business with Sinclaire Enterprises.

The 1980s brought Augie Sinclaire the wealth he craved, and the university, satisfied with the steady returns of its investments, continued its dealings with Augustin Sinclaire Enterprises. As each Sinclaire check made its way back to the university, Father Hugh Joyce grew in stature and importance. He basked in adulation and admiration, protected in his identity of priest and scholar.

"Came in handy that you could just pick up and go south whenever you wanted, right Hughie? 'Missionary work' you used to call it. Ha! What a crock!"

Hugh rubbed his eyelids trying to relieve the burning sensation he was feeling. His fingers grazed his chin, and he felt the rough growth on his jaw. His tongue was coated with bitter spittle. He couldn't remember when he had last eaten.

"Do you believe in ghosts, Señora?"

The priest's words startled Luz, but she responded to his question without hesitating.

"*Sí.* You know that we call them *espantos,* don't you? I still see my mother's ghost, and others, too. But mostly, I see my grandfather's *espanto.* He's with me almost always. Especially during the night."

"Are you afraid of him?"

"*Sí* ... I mean *no* ... what I mean is that I think that ghosts are really our memories, the ones that we don't, or can't, let go. When those memories frighten us, we think that it's the *espantos* that do it."

"Then you think that ghosts can haunt us?"

"'Haunt'? What's that, Padre, I don't understand."

"It means that if we let them, our ghosts come back to pick at us with their sharp edges. They never let us forget anything. They're everywhere, hiding around corners, crouching in little niches where we least expect them. They like to turn their spikes inside of us, trying to make us regret what we've done. And even when we're sorry; even when we're ready to do things in a different way, they still hound and punish us."

"Ah, sí, I know what you mean. And you're right. I mean about their waiting for us when we aren't ready to face them. Sometimes our *espantos* look like shadows, and sometimes they shine, but yes, they like to return, especially when we're alone."

Shocked by his openness with Luz, Father Hugh held his breath. He regretted having stirred her, and he hoped that she would return to her silent drowsiness. He waited a minute or two before he turned to looked at her. She was locked into her own thoughts, and she seemed far away. Father Hugh closed his eyes. They burned. His eyeballs seemed to be rolling in hot sand.

As the night hovered over San Salvador, moving toward its end, Hugh Joyce listened to the voice of the rector. Father Virgil's voice was a hoarse whisper and his words were strained but distinct. Another voice was interfering with Father Virgil's words, though. That voice soon was joined by another until the voices created an intolerable noise in Father Hugh's head.

"Shut up!"

Father Hugh looked into the emptiness, relieved that no one seemed to have heard his outburst. He again pressed his hands to his forehead, hoping that he might fall asleep. He tried reciting a psalm, but he was unable to call up even one although he knew many by heart. Instead he uttered fragments that collided with one another. His verses were a mesh of disconnected lines and words.

"I am aware of my faults, Oh, God...I have my sin constantly in mind...having sinned against none other than you...Death's terrors assail me, fear and trembling descend on me...Horror overwhelms me...Oh, for the wings of a dove to fly away and find rest...Take pity on me, God, as they harry me, pressing their attacks...My opponents harry me, hordes coming in to attack... ."

"Hugh! Listen to me. I'm not your enemy, I never was. You made it worse on your own. How could you have done what you did? Wasn't it bad enough that you made yourself a part of all this death and suffering?"

Father Hugh had to admit that he had messed things up even though he had been given the chance to make things right. He remembered now that it had been raining the night Father Virgil tapped at his door. When he entered he held papers in his trembling hands, and without saying a word, he passed the letter to Father Hugh who stiffly read its contents.

"Dear Father Virgil, I feel pained to be the one to inform you of Father Hugh Joyce's involvement in... ."

The letter detailed names, dates, and the amounts of money involved in each illegal deal. It provided the place of meetings and items discussed by Augie and Hugh and the others responsible in dealings that spanned years. There were pages crammed with accusations against the priest, telling of his direct involvement in the weapon business. The letter recounted the many trips taken by him to San Salvador to barter and settle deals, all with money finagled from the university.

Father Virgil found the accusation preposterous, impossible to believe. Before he had confronted Hugh, he had been convinced that it was a joke, or evidence of envy, even the work of a resentful student. Hugh, however, took a long time reading the contents of the letter, much longer than Father Virgil had expected. When Hugh finally raised his gaze, the rector saw fear in his eyes and he noticed his trembling hands.

Hugh denied it all, declaring that it was nonsense, a prank, or, worse, the intent of someone who wanted him disgraced in the eyes of the university. Hugh spoke rapidly, nervously stumbling over words, mumbling things unrelated to the accusation. He brought up Mr. Sinclaire's generosity, reminding Father Virgil of the insult to which Augie would be subjected if the accusations contained in the letter ever reached his ears. Besides, Hugh was a priest, he insisted to his superior, a man who had lived as conscientiously as possible, always mindful of his vows, and this dirty business would clearly be a breach of everything he represented.

Father Virgil left in turmoil, unconvinced by the younger priest's responses. Hugh's words had been hollow, and they had failed to explain the fear in his eyes. His hands had trembled without stopping, and his face never regained its natural color, and even though the rector had initially thought that the possibility of Hugh's involvement was beyond belief, he now felt grave misgivings.

After several days of reflection, Father Virgil decided to speak directly with Augustin Sinclaire. To his confusion, Sinclaire appeared to be expecting him. In his usual off-hand manner, Sinclaire admitted responsibility for the illegal enterprise in which Hugh Joyce was involved. He even willingly exposed more details, doing it arrogantly and sarcastically, while he nibbled on the tip of a long cigar.

Father Virgil was shocked, especially when he saw that Sinclaire's admission was not, as he would have expected, prompted by guilt or shame. On the contrary, he was boastful and he seemed to relish the moment. He mockingly pointed out that the university was also involved. Everyone, from the president down to the newest professor, was now culpable of the business of peddling death, he said. Sinclaire reminded Father Virgil that the university had not only accepted and used his donations, but had reinvested its own monies in support of the business they were now discussing. The university had done so, not once or twice, but consistently over ten years.

"So, Father Rector, if you have the balls to blow the whistle, good luck! Be my guest."

"You wrote the letter, didn't you?" Father Virgil asked.

"Why, Father Rector, you're not as stupid as Hughie thinks you are."

Father Virgil felt the sting of Sinclaire's sarcasm. He was offended by the implication that Hugh obviously had expressed an opinion regarding him.

"Why, in God's name, did you do it? I thought Hugh Joyce was your friend?"

"My friend? You must be joking! I would sooner be friends with a shark. Remember, Father, that I've known Hughie since we were just kids with snot running down our noses. Believe me, I know, he's a shark! His only friend is Hugh Joyce. Now, if you're asking why I wrote that letter, the answer is simple. First, Hugh's getting too big for his britches. He needs to be brought down a peg or two. You're the guy to do just that. Second, I'm bored with this whole damned thing. Oh, now, don't misunderstand me. I'm not bored with the moola. I wasn't dropped on my head when I was a kid. No, sir! What I mean is that I'm dying to see a little fireworks between Hugh and the big boys who run his life. Oh, I know damn well you'll never blow the whistle on the business. You guys are too smart for that. But what you will do—and I'll bet my money to your apples—is put that son of a bitch Hugh in his place. He deserves to... ."

Augie's voice trailed off when he saw Father Virgil stand and wordlessly leave the office. He was disappointed because he had wanted to tell Hugh's superior how much he hated the man everyone assumed was his best friend. Sinclaire yearned to tell the whole world how much he had grown to despise Hugh because of his arrogance, and more than anything, he wanted to reveal that he hated Hugh because he had shunned him when he had needed him most. He was willing to give anything to see Hugh humiliated and disgraced.

Father Virgil returned to the Residence where he spent the rest of the day in prayer. He was afraid, and he didn't know what to do, but that evening he returned to Hugh's room.

"The university's ties with Sinclaire must be severed immediately. It's your responsibility to see this accomplished without tarnishing the reputation of the university or anyone in it," Father Virgil commanded.

A deep silence wrapped itself wround the two men. When Father Virgil spoke again his voice was calm.

"You must resign from your position in the university at once," he ordered. "Sickness—your own, or someone else's—can be the excuse. Anything will do, but your action must be immediate."

Hugh refused to speak but his eyes betrayed rage and fear. The rector, seeing that the younger priest had nothing to say, turned and left the room. When he returned to his office, he wrote Hugh a brief letter: "As your superior, and in the name of obedience, I command you to cease and desist from the business in which you have been engaged for ten years. You are to do so immediately. I will see to it that you are transfered to another community as quickly as is conveniently possible."

Now, the cramped shelter only intensified Hugh's memory, and he clasped his hands over his eyes, trying to block out Father Virgil's image. Hot tears flooded his eyes. He felt that his throat was on fire, and that he was about to choke on his tongue. They were crowding in on him, all of them: Augie, Virgil, his father, his mother and others, every one of them pointing long, bony fingers at him. Behind them, Hugh thought he saw several Salvadorans peering in his direction. He rubbed his eyes. Were they the same ones who had been huddling in the shelter? Why were they staring at him? He heard them murmuring, whispering among themselves, wagging their uncombed, disheveled heads in agreement about something concerning him. Hugh shut his eyes so tightly that a blinding light flashed under his eyelids as he relived his most difficult moments.

He recalled that he had found Father Virgil's order impossible to fulfill. To have resigned from the university would have alerted Hugh's enemies. They would have probed and asked questions until the truth would have been discovered. He then would have been the object of mockery and disgust. Underlying his fear of humiliation, furthermore, had been probability of imprisonment.

Hugh had decided not to obey Father Virgil's order. Instead, he had confronted him. The two men had argued violently, with Hugh asserting that he would not be a scapegoat. He had threatened to reveal that the university, not he, was the guilty party. He had reminded Father Virgil that if he were exposed, it would be they, the priests, who would hear the full brunt of the accusation. A major scandal would be the result.

Hugh, enraged, was aggressive and hostile with Father Virgil. He shouted at him even though he saw the old man's face grow pale and twitch with pain. At one point, Hugh had raised a clenched fist, jabbing the air close to the other priest's face. He had lowered his hand only when Father Virgil collapsed in his chair. When Hugh had left the rector's office, he had been quaking with anger, and his face had been drained of its usual color. The next day the community of priests awakened to the notice that their rector had died of a massive heart attack.

In the shelter, Hugh now felt as if his lungs were deflating. He could barely breathe. Father Virgil's slumped body appeared in the darkness at his feet. Hugh's eyes bulged with horror as they had when he had looked at the rector's body shortly after his death.

Outside, a new wave of helicopters scooped down over the shelter. A barrage of missiles and bombs tore at the city of the Savior with jaws of steel and fire. In the bleak darkness, the stench of terror mingled with stifling heat as Father Hugh Joyce wrestled with the *espantos* that were tormenting him.

PART FOUR

Yahweh asked Cain, "Where is your brother...? What have you done?...Now be accursed..."

Genesis, Chapter 4

I

As Luz and the priest huddled in the bunker, Bernabé crouched against a dirt embankment staring at the dark sky. There was a sudden barrage of explosions, and he tried to shrink deeper into the dirt. "¡Madre!" he heard himself say.

Bernabé waited a few moments before he glanced at his watch noting that it was almost dawn. He hoped that the signal would be given soon so that he could lead the guerrilla assault on military headquarters. The building was enveloped in silence, and to all appearance the guards slept, seemingly unaware that they had been singled out as one of the guerrillas' objective. Bernabé and the rest of his companions knew, however, that the silence and the dark windows were a ploy. It was unlikely that the Guard was not prepared. Bernabé expected a bloody confrontation, but in the meantime, all was quiet.

His thoughts drifted back to his early days with his compañeros, to the day he was promoted to sergeant for having guided the refugees across the Río Sumpul. He remembered that those days had been difficult for him, particularly when he had realized that now he would never get to be a priest. That was when he had persuaded himself that instead of peace, the gospel preached by Jesus was really one of murder and torture. Bernabé later admitted to himself that he had falsely convinced himself that as a guerrilla he could do more for his brothers and sisters than as a priest.

He shifted his body as his muscles began to feel the pressure of crouching. He returned to his thoughts, remembering that his commitment to killing had been frail from the beginning, and that it had weakened each time he put a bullet into a soldier's head, or participated in torturing a spy. He was hounded by the thought that the victims were his brothers, Salvadorans like him, and that each time he killed, he became less human.

As he awaited the signal to attack, his thoughts shifted to his mother whose image was always with him. He didn't ever wonder if he would recognize her if he were to see her after so many years. Nor did he consider that she would have difficulty recognizing him. His face, once joyful, had become gloomy. Where it had been oval shaped and soft, it was now flat and stiff. His forehead was furrowed by wrinkles that resembled cracks in stone, and his cheekbones had thinned and become prominent. Bernabé's round mouth had become a straight line, its corners creased by tiny, lingering downward curves, which reflected his constant sadness. The eyes he inherited from his mother had long before dulled, betraying cynicism and dejection.

The source of Bernabé's disenchantment came from the realization that destiny had turned his life into a cruel joke, casting him into a world of terror and violence and disappointment. He was obsessed with the fact that life had robbed him of his dream of living out Christ's gospel by ministering to the needs of those around him. He and his compañeros had become assassins, changing little by little each day, becoming as monstrous as the enemy.

When he had first come to the mountain, Bernabé had been a young man filled with optimism. Now he was a melancholic old man, withdrawn and prematurely aged by the crimes and horrors that he had both seen and committed. He had allowed himself to become a contradiction. He had accepted what he thought was his fate and thus, had become a murderer.

Each act of terror had increased Bernabé's depression and isolation. In the beginning, especially, his nights had been filled with guilt, but in time, his sentiments were dulled by the incessant sight of blood. He recalled the incident at the Río Sumpul which had made him a hero. There had been other times, other places, however, where he had not been as fortunate. He remembered the slaughter in the town of Mozote—its date was no longer clear—where soldiers had slit the throats of the men of the village, machine-gunned the women, and burned the babies and children in the town church.

Stark images of atrocities were jumbled up in Bernabé's memory, and it was only with difficulty that he sorted them out. What happened in one village, merged with what happened in other towns. Pictures of starving men were stamped on every one of Bernabé's waking moments. He was haunted by the vision of a mother holding her child's bullet-riddled body in her arms. Her elbows dripped blood, and she moaned and wept. Stunned out of her mind, she had let out a lament, a mournful cradle song for her dead child.

Lempa, Chalatenango, Guazapa, San Vicente, Santa Tecla, even the steps leading to the Cathedral in San Salvador were now echoes of explosions, screams and moans. One episode was as painful as the last. Suddenly, Bernabé's memories focused on an incident of several years before. It involved his compañero Nestor Solís.

"Nestor! Don't do it, please!" he found himself saying as he relived the horror once again.

Nestor, Bernabé and a few of the compañeros had stumbled onto the campsite of three soldiers. The guerrillas were startled to find the men napping, but that had given them the advantage of being the first to take action. By the time the soldiers reacted to the enemy's presence, the compañeros had their weapons pointed at each man's head. The soldiers raised their shaking hands above their heads as they attempted to persuade the guerrillas not to execute them.

"Compañero, I'm a Salvadoran like you. I have a mother, and a father, and a wife. I'm the father of... ."

"¡Cállate, hijo de tu puta madre!"

Nestor's rifle butt put an end to the soldier's stuttering. Jets of blood and splinters of shattered teeth spurted on Nestor's face. The soldier jerked back as he fell on his haunches, his hands covering his bleeding face. The two others, eyes opened wide with terror, remained riveted to their original position on the ground. Nestor got even closer to the writhing soldier. He kicked him in the stomach with all the force of his leg so that the soldier rolled over, contorted with pain.

Muttering obscenities, Nestor kicked the soldier's haunches again, aiming at his kidneys. Bernabé and the other guerrillas looked on in silence. For years they had assisted Nestor in his search for the soldiers who had brutalized his sisters, and they had gotten accustomed to watching him vent his rage on whichever soldier happened to be in his power. They assumed that this was just another such incident.

But as Nestor's eyes moved from the prone soldier to the one next to him, the guerrillas sensed that this time Nestor had found his real target. He paused, startled as he crouched closer to the man. The brown skin, the slanted eyes, the high cheekbones, and the scar that stretched from the man's nose to his right ear, betrayed his identity.

"¡Hijo de tu puta madre! ¡Ya te encontré!"

With a rifle blow that leveled the soldier to his knees, Nestor took hold of the mans's head, digging his fingers into his face. He twisted the soldier's head, jerking it back and forth as if his neck had been soft rubber. With the soldier's head still gripped tightly in his hands, Nestor looked around at Bernabé. Then he let out a scream that reverberated through the small valley. Nestor's lips were wet with saliva as he stared at his fellow guerrillas.

Removing one of his hands from his victim's jaw, Nestor pulled a knife from his belt. As he lifted it in the air, its blade glinted in the sun's waning rays. Savoring the moment, he held the blade in front of the terrified soldier's eyes. The man trembled as sweat poured from his face and body.

"¡Cabrón!" Nestor hissed the word through clenched teeth.

The soldier attempted to utter something, but was interrupted by a vicious kick to the groin. The man doubled over in pain. Nestor then forced the man back to his knees and muttered, "Look, pig! Do you remember me? Try to think, it might save your life!"

Nestor glared at the soldier in silence, now and then making gestures with his face, grimaces meant to coax the soldier to speak. The soldier finally acknowledged with a nod of his head that he remembered. This was the signal for Nestor. Holding the knife directly in front of the man's eyes, Nestor spoke.

"Pig, do you know what happens to a man when that little sack we have down there is punctured? Do you have an idea of how much blood comes out of a man when that pouch is split apart?"

Despite his own acts of terrorism, Bernabé now lost his nerve because he knew what was coming.

"¡Por Dios!...Nestor...just blow his brains out...stop this torture!" Bernabé's voice was choked and halting.

"Shut up, Bernabé! The rest of you, keep away! Keep your distance, or as your mother lives, I swear that it's your own brains that I'll blow out!"

Turning his attention to the soldier, Nestor smashed his boot against the man's shoulder, knocking him on his back. The soldier was crying, imploring for his life.

"Take off his pants! Hold him down, legs spread apart!"

The man began to shriek in horror as two of the compañeros obeyed the orders. Then with a single gash, Nestor cut the man's scrotum. He shoved the testes into the man's twisted mouth.

Bernabé was compelled to act. Clutching his weapon he approached the man who was still twitching. He placed the rifle against the soldier's forehead and pulled the trigger, then he shot each of the other soldiers in the face. After this he began to quiver. Bernabé's arms and legs shook as he felt a wave of disgust for himself and his compañeros.

Several explosions ripped through the darkness blowing away the entrance of army headquarters. Bernabé was jarred back into the present remembering that the detonations signaled the guerrilla squads to advance. Massive blasts followed, making the earth quake. Clenching a machine gun, he pounced forward leading his men and ordering them to fan out, and to enter the fortress building at will.

Slipping around a corner, Bernabé slithered through a door that had been flung open. As he made his way up a dark stairway, he was suddenly surprised by the touch of cold steel against the back of his head.

"¡No se mueva!"

The order was a whisper close to Bernabé's ear. He froze as a hand gripped his arm, removing his weapon without speaking, the hand nudged him up the stairs, and into a dark room in which he sensed the presence of others.

"Silencio".

Outside the shooting stopped suddenly. In its place there was an ominous silence. Eventually Bernabé heard another voice.

"We're in control, *mi Coronel.* They were all bark and no bite."

Bernabé heard a hushed laughing in the darkness, then the lights were turned on. The barrel of the pistol he had felt at his head was finally lowered. He looked around. Blinking from the brilliance of the neon lights, he saw a large room with maps on the walls. Telephones and other equipment for communications were spread out on several desks.

When Bernabé's eyes adjusted to the light, he looked beyond the soldier who had captured him. He saw a tall man dressed in the field uniform of a colonel. The officer walked across the room, approaching the prisoner. He stood several inches above Bernabé. The man's complexion was milk-white, his hair was the color of gold, and his piercing eyes were pale blue. Colonel Delcano's lips were drawn into a straight, arrogant line as he gazed at Bernabé.

The overhead fluorescent lights clicked off, and the faded morning light filtered through the garrison's barred windows.

II

Colonel Delcano smiled arrogantly when he faced Bernabé, but his smile veiled the torment raging in his heart. Thanks to his collection of photographs, his brother's face was engraved on his mind, and he knew right away who this prisoner was. Fortune had placed him in his hands. A lifetime of anger and jealousy surged within the colonel's heart, and his first impulse was to execute his brother on the spot, in spite of the witnesses. Nothing could stop him. There was a war going on, and here was a guerrilla leader. Lucio Delcano decided to wait, however.

"Put him in a cell. Keep him there until I give you new orders!" The colonel returned to his office to plan his next step. Alone in his office, he sat at his desk, absentmindedly biting his upper lip as he concentrated. He felt the palms of his hands wet with perspiration as he pondered what to do with his brother. Then his mother's image crossed his mind. He had received a brief message from one of his agents stating that the woman, Luz Delcano, had been observed wandering through the streets of the city during the fighting. He gazed at the oversized city map hanging on the wall opposite his desk, realizing that after all these years, his mother and his brother were now within his reach. The colonel sat back in his chair, his hands set in a triangle under his chin. He knew that he would have his brother executed in the end. Yet, at that moment, he could not rid himself of an apprehension, a shakiness unknown to him.

He remained at his desk, his face stiff, and his body oddly poised. His blond hair looked white against the fluorescent lamps. The clock ticked, but the colonel had lost track of time. When he finally closed his eyes, pausing for a few seconds, he was aware of a fly that buzzed in the chamber's silent air. Slowly he picked up one of the telephones.

"Call in the Lieutenant."

"En seguida, *Coronel.*"

When the officer entered the office, Delcano waved him to a chair. "I have a detail to request of you before day's end."

"*Mi Coronel*, you know that I'm always at your disposition."

The colonel stared at him without betraying the intense distaste the man's abject subservience produced in him. "Do you know of the capture of the guerrilla leader?" he questioned.

"*Sí, mi Coronel.*"

"Good. He seems to stand out from the rest...more intelligent... better prepared. The point is that I'm requesting that you execute him as soon as possible. There's the possibility that an attempt to liberate him might take place."

The lieutenant stared at the colonel.

"What's the matter, Teniente? You seem surprised. Certainly, it's not the first time that you've been ordered to execute a traitor."

"But...he's your brother...!" The soldier blurted out the words.

Colonel Delcano was stunned by the lieutenant's words. Struggling to maintain his composure, he immediately understood that the picture had suddenly changed; the man facing him had to be eliminated. Without betraying the anger he felt at this unexpected turn in his calculations, Lucio Delcano was able to respond in a serene, controlled voice.

"Yes, he is my brother."

The lieutenant was at a loss for words. He could only stare at the colonel.

"Teniente, you'll perform your duty where you think best. El Playón would probably offer the best conditions for such a mission. But first, we'll speak with him here."

The lieutenant was showing signs of increasing nervousness and confusion. He shifted his body in the chair, and his hands were clasped tightly on his lap.

"*Mi Coronel*, here? You and I?"

The idea of interrogating a suspect in the colonel's office frightened the lieutenant. He was unsure of what the consequences might be for him.

"I confess, *mi Coronel*, that I'm not quite sure of what you mean. Regarding what matters are we to question the prisoner? If I may be so disrespectful as to say that it's highly unlikely that he'll disclose information regarding the guerrillas, even under rigorous interrogation. And if that's what we want, well then, I must go even further and say that in that case we need someone trained in the delicacies of extracting information from a recalcitrant subject. If you understand what I mean."

"Indeed I understand your meaning, Teniente. You are the one who does not understand mine. The conversation," he said the word sarcastically, "between my brother and me will not be an interrogation. We have things to say to one another. You merely will be the witness."

Colonel Delcano paused long enough for the words to sink into the lieutenant's mind. "You'll be a witness and, of course, later on the executioner," he said firmly.

The colonel's face was a mask. The lieutenant began to shiver. "Sí, *mi Coronel,* whatever you say. Tell me the time, and I'll be here."

The colonel looked at his watch. It was slightly past eleven in the morning. "Be here in exactly two hours," he commanded. "Please be prompt. I'll see to it that the prisoner is here by the time you arrive."

The lieutenant rose, saluted and left the office. Then the colonel rang for the orderly.

"Why are the telephones silent? Are the connections in order?"

"Sí, *mi Coronel,* but the city is quiet. The fighting appears to have stopped in most of the barrios. Nothing new has occurred."

"Very well. Keep me informed."

The colonel hunched over his massive desk with his face buried in his hands for a long time. After a while he glanced at his watch and saw that it was almost one o'clock. He called his aide into the inner office.

"Bring me the prisoner. When the lieutenant arrives, show him in. After that, you are not to interrupt us under any circumstances. Only a communication from the president's office will be received."

"Sí, *mi Coronel.*"

Once alone, he went to a filing case and removed two files. He opened the folder containing photographs of Bernabé's early years with Luz. For longer than he realized, Lucio sifted through the pile, pushing pictures aside with his long index finger. He was looking for one in particular. The photograph showed the boy dressed in white, standing at the entrance of a church, accompanied by his mother and a priest. Delcano picked up the photo, holding it delicately, as if afraid that it would fall apart. He saw that his fingers trembled lightly. He allowed the picture to slip through his fingers onto the desk. He turned to the other file containing details of Luz's search for Bernabé.

There was a rap on the door. The colonel tensed.

"¡Adelante!"

The door opened. The lieutenant, who was carrying a machine gun, was the first to enter. He was followed by two armed guards who shoved the prisoner toward the center of the room. Bernabé was handcuffed. His face was sallow and haggard from sleeplessness, but he stood erect, showing no signs of fear or intimidation. With an authoritative glance, Colonel Delcano dismissed the two guards, who stiffly turned, quietly closing the door behind them.

"Remove the handcuffs."

Colonel Delcano's voice was calm, cold. It did not betray his inner turmoil. The lieutenant obeyed immediately.

"Be seated!"

The order was aimed at Bernabé who took a seat. As he looked at the colonel, his eyes filled with disdain. The lieutenant also sat, placing himself behind Bernabé while he balanced the machine gun on his lap.

Colonel Delcano hovered behind his desk.

"Your name and rank!"

"Cura. Capitán."

"I want your true name!"

The colonel was impatient; calculations of an entire lifetime had to be carried out within a short time. Bernabé, however, remained calm as he glared defiantly at his interrogator. Finally, he said,"My rank is that of captain, and my name is *Cura."*

Delcano felt incensed at the prisoner's boldness, and his mouth flooded with bitter saliva as he strained to fight off the impulse to slap Bernabé. He overcame his anger, however, instinctively knowing that to take the lead in the process he had to put Bernabé on the defensive.

"Your name is Bernabé, and the surname your mother claimed for you and for herself is Delcano. Am I not correct, Bernabé?"

The colonel emphasized Bernabé's name mockingly, taking pleasure in the surprise his brother was unable to hide. Sensing Bernabé's confusion, he felt invigorated.

"Well, Bernabé Delcano," he smirked, "since I know your name, I want you to know mine. I'm Lucio Delcano."

Bernabé was unable to mask his shock, and the colonel was satisfied to see his brother's body stiffen as if an iron rod had been rammed up his spine. Lucio spoke slowly, relishing each word, as he watched the movements and flutters in his brother's face. The colonel pulled up a chair, and sat very close to Bernabé, placing his face so that his nose nearly grazed his brother's cheeks. Bernabé felt his brother's hot breath on his skin. Breathing with difficulty that increased by the second, Lucio Delcano whispered these words, "I'm your brother. Your mother conceived me when she fornicated with her grandfather."

He paused, waiting for the words to take effect. Bernabé attempted to look away from the colonel's intense eyes.

"Look at me! I said, look at me! The two of them made me what I am! Then she wound up selling me, abandoning me so she could lead the life of a slut. That's how she got you. I'll tell you how. By betraying the woman who took her into her house, by fornicating with that woman's husband. That's how! Yes! That's you, just another bastard...like me."

Bernabé kept quiet, this time glaring straight at his brother, his pupils distended. Perspiration was seeping from his hair and face, and the colonel could not tell if the drops that coursed down Bernabé's chin, dripping onto his clenched hands, were tears or sweat.

"Delcano! You are *not* a Delcano! You're a Grijalva! Impostor! Liar!"

The colonel's voice trembled with a rage that intensified until he could hardly breathe. His words were hoarse, nearly unintelligible. Then all of a sudden his throat dried up, unexpectedly forcing him into silence, making him unable to articulate the words that were still burning in his mind.

In his fantasies, Lucio had imagined that he would one day horrify his brother with the information he had amassed over the years. He had planned to crush Bernabé's spirit by telling him of their mother's depravity. Oddly, though, he was now physically incapable of expressing those words. He knew he was drained of strength. He even feared that he would crumble under the power of his brother's defiant eyes.

Bernabé silently stared at his brother, no longer attempting to look away, and as if in a trance, both men remained silent, motionless, their gaze interlocked. The ticking of the clock measured the silence.

It was the colonel who first lowered his eyes. He turned to the lieutenant and, with a nod of his head, ordered him to remove the prisoner. The lieutenant left his chair and approached the prisoner. "¡Vámonos!"

Colonel Delcano sat motionless in his chair long after the door closed. He listened to his brother's fading footsteps until they became an echo in his memory.

III

"You can stop shivering, Pal. It's over for the time being."

Augie's presence was real to the priest. The voice seemed to have taken a concrete form. Hugh saw Augie slumped on the floor against the wall of the shelter. His artificial leg stuck out awkwardly while the other leg was pulled up against his body. He rested his elbow against this leg and squeezed a half-smoked cigar between his stubby fingers.

"Hey! Do you think we're in the smoking section of this dump?"

He chuckled at his joke, but Father Hugh was silent. His face was haggard and his lips were pressed tightly against his teeth.

"How long has it been since you last did business with the colonel, Hughie?"

"You mean we, don't you?"

"All right, Kid. Have it your way. How long has it been since we did business with the guy?"

Father Hugh didn't want to talk. He thought that if he kept quiet the voice would go away.

"Well? When was it that you last talked to the bastard?"

"Look, Augie, I don't want to talk to you anymore. I'm getting out of this place, and I'm heading right back home. I don't know what I'm doing here in the first place."

"Just a minute, Buddy. No one's going anywhere until I say so."

Augie's words had a paralyzing effect on Hugh. He felt as if his neck were pinned to the wall by an invisible nail. He looked over to Luz but she was silent, and her head was still reclined on her knees.

"Come on, Hughie boy. When was the last time you danced with our friend the colonel?"

"This time a year ago."

The colonel's face suddenly appeared. He was looking intently at the priest as he did whenever they met. The white face was a mask.

His pale hand was offering the priest the expensive cigar Hugh always smoked when he finalized a deal with Colonel Delcano.

"Hugh, you knew that the colonel was involved in the death of the old Archbishop back in 1980."

"No, I didn't!" The priest 's voice was raspy, on the verge of cracking.

"Ha! You're such goddamn liar! Sure, you knew it. I knew it. And I knew that you knew. We just didn't talk about it, did we, old chum? Mainly because we just didn't give a shit."

Hugh was quiet for a long time remembering that he had suspected Colonel Delcano's involvement in the assassination but had turned his attention away from the matter at the time.

"You knew, didn't you, Hugh?"

"What difference does it make now, Augie? What's the point? It's been almost ten years! What's the difference?"

"It makes a lot of difference, Pal. Believe me."

Augie paused. He seemed to be reflecting. After a while, he asked, *"Are you sorry?"*

Hugh's head whipped around. He was muttering under his breath.

"Sorry? For what? What are you talking about? I didn't have anything to do with anyone's death. Back off, Augie, you're making me sick! You're a fine one to talk about being sorry."

"I know, Hugh. I have no right to ask you this."

The priest was surprised by Augie's words, and especially by his tone. Hugh thought he heard humility, even remorse in Augie's voice.

"Hugh, did you know that the colonel was behind the murder of a lot of people?"

"No! I didn't know any such thing. I had work that kept me from meddling in other people's business. Remember? I was busy doing my job at the university and... ."

"What, my friend? The business of murder was too insignificant for you? It was for me and I admit it."

Father Hugh knew that there had been several murders, all of them unresolved. He was thinking that some of them had been Americans. "Look, Augie, if people died—and I'm not ready to say I know who was responsible—they shared in some of the blame. You tell me, what do people expect when they stick their nose into politics?"

"I don't know what they expect. That's not the point. They were murdered, and we knew who was responsible, and we did business with that murderer. That's the point, Hugh. Don't you see?"

The priest was on the edge of panic, he felt the shelter becoming intolerable. He looked over to where Luz was leaning against the wall, and he saw that she was sleeping. He made a move to stand. He wanted to run to Colonel Delcano who could make sure that he got back home.

"Are you sorry, Hugh?"

Augie's voice was a whisper pressing Hugh's body back down onto the concrete floor.

"There you go again! Sorry? Sorry for what?"

"For all those deaths, Pal."

"No! I'm not sorry! Why should I be? I had nothing to do with... ."

"Yes you did! We both did! We made the Colonel successful; we saw to it that he got away with what he wanted. We didn't pull the trigger, but we sure as Hell made it possible. I'm sorry for it all, Hugh, why can't you be?"

"Leave me alone!"

The air in the shelter was nauseating Father Hugh. He looked around at the people who had been lumped together during the night. He saw that they were moving. Shadows were crossing from one side of the place to the other in silence. Hugh focused his eyes on one of them, convinced that he was staring at him.

"They're suffering, Hugh."

"Who's suffering?"

"They are. The ones you're looking at. They don't know it, but they might as well be dead. Just like me."

Hugh could no longer endure Augie's voice, so he decided to leave the shelter to find Colonel Delcano.

"Hugh, wait! Are you sorry?"

"No! I'm not sorry."

"Are you sure you're not sorry, Hugh? Not even for what you did to Father Virgil?"

"Damn it, Augie! I've done nothing to regret."

As Father Hugh spoke, he looked at Augie. The vision was so real that he felt he could actually touch his outstretched leg. It looked natural, not stiff and artificial. Hugh looked up at Augie's face and shoulders. He saw that he had something draped over his shoulders. It hung on him like a priest's stole, and his head was reclined against his hand as if he were listening. The priest began to laugh at the idea of Augie hearing his confession.

"Hey, Augie, what the Hell do you think you're doing? I'm the priest, not you, remember?"

Hugh laughed louder. His laughter was hollow, nearing hysteria.

He stopped abruptly and got to his feet. He looked at Luz. She was still crouching, and she didn't look up at the priest.

"Never mind, Hugh, leave her alone. She'll be along in a minute. Come on. I need to show you a few things before we can leave."

Father Hugh pulled back in an attempt to put space between himself and the voice. "Look Augie, let's get this thing straight," he emphasized, "I'm not going with you. I'm going out into the daylight where I'll be able to put my brains back together again, and then it's back home."

Father Hugh made his way toward the exit of the shelter. He had to maneuver himself around the crouching bodies, carefully going around some of them, creeping over others. He wondered why they were all so still, why they didn't show signs of wanting to return to the streets and to their homes.

Once outside the building, the priest squinted in the grayish early morning light. He rubbed his eyes, blinked and looked around him, breathing deeply, grateful to be out of the rancid air of the shelter. The street was filled with rubble, and he saw several bodies lying under pieces of concrete and trash. Their limbs were twisted and they were beginning to bloat. Hugh turned to make his way toward the center of the city, and from there to Colonel Delcano's office.

There was an eerie silence. The wind was blowing through the shattered walls of buildings, creating a sucking sound that echoed softly. Father Hugh seemed to be the only living person left in the city. At first he walked as quickly as his stiff legs could manage, his footsteps making a crunching sound that bounced off the walls. Then, wherever the streets were not clogged with rubble or pocked with holes, Hugh ran as fast as his legs would permit.

He was relieved when he finally saw two men. Then he began to meet more people, men and women who seemed to be heading in the same direction. The number kept growing. Soon it became a large crowd. Hugh decided to follow it figuring that he was bound to find someone to help him.

The streets filled with the murmur of voices, and the people surrounding Father Hugh were agitated. They exchanged comments that were out of his hearing. He sensed, however, that something important enough to halt the fighting of the past days had occurred. A battered ambulance, its red light flashing and siren blaring, careened by the priest. It was headed in the direction in which the crowd was moving. The ambulance was followed by a military truck loaded with soldiers, prompting Hugh to run in the hopes of catching up with them. He knew that one of them would put him in contact with the colonel.

When he turned the corner, he found himself facing the wide entrance of a residence. Its small garden was filled with soldiers and ambulance attendants. Hugh pressed his way through the on-lookers. His eyes caught view of a man's body, still wearing his underclothes, stretched out on the grass. As Hugh looked up, he saw a priest standing over the body. The priest was actually a bishop, he realized. Hugh squeezed even closer, looking beyond the corpse. There were other bodies, and their heads seemed to have been blown open .

"Jesus... !"

The word escaped Hugh's lips. His heart began to race.

"¡Son sacerdotes. Todos!"

Father Hugh shuddered at the sound of the voice, and his head whipped around to see who had spoken. It had been a woman. He questioned her.

"¿Sacerdotes? ¿Está segura, Señora?"

"Sí, Señor. "

A lump was knotting in Hugh's throat as saliva caught in his mouth. The blood in his head pounded against his temples, and his hands were shaking uncontrollably. Voices of on-lookers pressed into his ears, buzzing shrilly, and he felt that he was going to faint.

"What's the matter, Hugh?"

Hugh was caught off guard by the voice. Augie came to him during the dark hours of the night, never during the day.

"Sorry, Buddy, I didn't mean to spook you. You'd better relax though because there are still a few more things we have to do before it's all over."

Father Hugh was stunned. He didn't know what to say or think. As he looked over his shoulder his eyes narrowed in surprise when he saw Luz leaning against the concrete wall of the garden. Her arms were serenely folded over her chest, and she seemed to be observing the dead bodies. When he left the shelter he had thought that he would never see her again, but now he felt he needed to go over to her. However, he was stopped again by the voice.

"Were they involved in politics, too? Seems to me you said a while ago that was the reason that people got plugged."

Hugh's mouth was clamped shut. His jaw had locked.

"Hugh, look over there. No, not there. More to your right...over there by the one with the shoes on. You got it. What do you see on the ground, my friend?"

Hugh couldn't answer the question even though his eyes were riveted on the used shell casings.

"You recognize the gauge, don't you, Buddy? Yes, you do, don't play dumb! It's identical to the junk we peddled down here. We might as well have loaded the weapons ourselves."

Father Hugh attempted to lurch toward the gate with the intention of running away, but something held him back.

"Not so fast, Pal. You're going in the wrong direction. Come with me."

Hugh found himself surrendering. He turned once more to take a final look at the murdered priests, but the crowd blocked his view. Hugh, however, saw that Luz was just behind him, and that she was standing with her hands stuffed into the side pockets of her dress, while she turned her head, searching in different directions. She looked like a lost child.

"Señora, come with me!"

She joined the priest, and together they walked the streets of San Salvador for hours, without pausing even to speak, staring wordlessly at ruins of homes, shattered streets, and burned tree stumps.

"Tell me Hugh, what do you smell? You always had a good sniffer."

"Nothing!"

"Yeh, you do. You just don't want to 'fess up to it. You're smelling the same thing I'm smelling. Rotting human flesh. Smells kind of sweet, doesn't it? You're smelling human shit, too. Did you know that most people do that when they're scared out of their wits? I mean, they actually crap in their pants. Could happen to you too, Pal."

Father Hugh was sickened by what he was seeing and hearing and smelling. The air was polluted by the stench of dead bodies and rancid sulphur. Maimed children with limbs missing sat crying for someone to help. Distraught mothers ran up and down the winding streets.

"We're a part of it all, and we did a good job, didn't we Hughie? And it's not over yet. There's more to come."

The priest knew his nerves were shattering. He felt that he and this strange woman had died, and that together they were walking the streets of Hell. Then he told himself that it would pass, that neither he nor the woman were dead, and that he was not insane. He muttered this over and again, saying that it was natural that he should be undergoing stress, and that few people could stand up to the horrors of what he had experienced over the past several hours.

Unable to convince himself, however, Hugh felt that he couldn't wait any longer. Leaving Luz behind, he began to run. At first he trotted, then he broke into a sprint. The priest ran from block to block, hoping that someone would help him find Colonel Delcano.

At last he found two guards. "Where can I find Colonel Delcano?" he asked them.

Hugh was out of breath, and he could hardly pronounce the words. One of the soldiers pointed in the direction of the Estado Mayor.

"Allí."

IV

"I'm sorry, Señor Joyce, but you cannot wait here any longer. The colonel cannot receive you until five this afternoon. Civilians are not allowed in this area for long periods of time. You will have to wait elsewhere."

Father Hugh rose from where he had been seated and dejectedly walked out of the outer offices of the Estado Mayor. When he stepped out on the street he again faced the city's destruction. Even though the streets were quiet, the air was still saturated with smoke and dust, and patrols of armed government troops were present everywhere.

As the priest stood on the rubble-strewn curb, uncertain as to which direction to take, he was startled when the building's heavy metal doors swung open with a loud noise. A military van lumbered out and stopped almost in front of him. Hugh's attention was caught by two soldiers as they emerged from behind the vehicle escorting a prisoner. The man's hands were handcuffed behind his back.

Hugh watched the soldiers shove the prisoner onto the flatbed of the van, slam the door behind him, and wait at attention until a lieutenant emerged from the building. The officer peered into the rear of the van, nodded, and climbed onto the passenger seat of the vehicle. The other soldiers jumped on the running board of the van, which slowly made its way toward a nearby hill.

Father Hugh turned away and walked, without direction. He saw that others too were wandering, moving without knowing where to go, or what to do. People walked in silence; a pall hung over them and their city. The priest made his way, often tripping over pieces of concrete and scattered rubbish, other times falling into potholes. His lungs and eyes ached from the contaminated air, and his stomach growled because he had gone without eating for so long.

Hugh walked aimlessly for a while before he realized that he had made his way to the heart of the city. He found himself facing the Cathedral. For a long time he stood staring at the concrete beneath his feet, his shoulders sagging, his legs wobbly and unsteady. After a few minutes, he decided to enter the building, thinking that he might find shelter. When he walked into the gloom he found that the church was filled with huddling, frightened people. The priest could hear the faint weeping and moaning of adults. He saw a child sprawled at the foot of one of the pillars. He could not tell if the child was asleep or dead. His eyes made out the figures of men crouched on the floor of the massive church. Women, bundled in soiled shawls, were seated in the pews.

"Santa María, llena eres de gracia..."

Buzzing tones of three or four people praying the rosary cut through the darkened interior of the Cathedral. Father Hugh leaned against a pillar, shaking his head in an attempt to clear his thoughts. Giving in to his fatigue, he allowed his body to slide slowly downward until he, too, was crouching on his haunches.

"...el Señor es contigo..."

The priest tried to pray, but he couldn't. He was thinking of how he had walked out on his community and his university hoping to find peace; instead, he had fallen into this snake pit. Now his only desire was to get out, to leave this Hell behind him, and never again to return to it. He also felt resentment welling up inside of him. He was angered at these people for allowing this Hell to exist.

"Bendita eres entre todas las mujeres..."

He was also resentful that Colonel Delcano had put him off for so many hours. Father Hugh had presumed that he would have been received immediately, and that as usual he would have been given top priority. He had always been treated well during his business trips, housed in the best hotel suite in the city and dined at the best restaurants. This sudden change in Colonel Delcano's attitude puzzled him.

"The colonel's giving you the cold shoulder, eh, Hughie?"

Father Hugh's heart almost stopped. Even though his impulse was to run from the voice, he shut his eyes. He could feel himself sweating.

"Come on, Hughie boy, open those peepers. You and I still have some things to talk about."

"Go away Augie! Leave me alone! Please! I don't have anything to say to you, not a single, goddamn thing!"

"Shame! Shame! Taking the name of the Lord in vain; and in His own

house no less! You ought to be ashamed of yourself, Father Hugh."

The priest sprang to his feet, and plunged into the darkness of the Cathedral toward its main altar. He stumbled over kneeling women and bumped against pews. He slipped once, scraping his knee against a sharp edge. Hugh scrambled up the main aisle hoping to rid himself of the sarcastic voice ringing in his ears.

"¡Padre Hugo! ¡Chssst! ¡Padre Hugo!"

Father Hugh heard someone hissing his name. At first he thought that it was Augie's voice, but when he turned he saw Luz seated on a bench. Her hair was more disheveled than ever. It stuck out in every direction, much of it clinging limply to her sweaty forehead. As Hugh's eyes became more accustomed to the gloom, he began to see that Luz's dress was even more soiled than it had been during their night in the shelter. Her feet were almost black with grime and dirt, and her hands were muddied as if she had been digging in dirt.

"Señora, what are you doing here? I thought I'd never see you again."

"I'm waiting for you, Padre Hugo. I'm glad you've arrived because I was beginning to lose patience."

"What do you mean? How could you have known I'd come here?"

Luz seemed distracted and she ignored the priest's questions. After a few moments, during which she looked around as if she were trying to locate someone in particular, she spoke.

"I have good news for you, Padrecito. I know where I can find Bernabé."

"You know where to find your son? Where? Who told you where he is?"

"Why are you surprised that I have finally found him, Padre? You know that I've spent years searching for him."

The woman fell silent for a moment. Her eyes were fevered, and she bit her lower lip as she concentrated.

"Padre, it was my comadre Aurora. You know, I told you about her last night. She came out of the barrio to tell me where I could find my son. He's up on El Playón. I don't know how she found out; she wouldn't tell me. But now that I know where Bernabé is for sure, I think I'm afraid. I wanted you to come with me, so I waited here. Come on Padre Hugo. Come with me, please. I'm very anxious."

Luz stood and, taking Father Hugh's hand, she carefully made her way around the crowd toward the main exit. She didn't let go of the priest's hand as they walked through the maze of littered streets. Her steps were confident and brisk; she knew where she was going.

The priest became nervous when he realized that they were heading in the direction of the mount where the prisoner had been taken.

"Where are we going, Señora? I have an appointment this afternoon. I can't go too far with you."

"You'll be back on time. I promise you Padre."

They walked in silence. Hugh could hear both his breath and Luz's as they walked for several blocks, turning corners, heading for the mount. The air began to smell, but the stench was different from the one hanging over the center of the city. This odor was of garbage, rotting and putrid. The breeze seemed to pick up as Luz and Father Hugh neared the hill, and with it, the nauseating stink of rot intensified.

Father Hugh was startled by something in the sky. He looked up, squinting in the grayish glare. He focused his eyes, realizing that he was looking at circling vultures. Fear gripped his heart.

"My God! Where are we going, Señora?"

Luz didn't answer the priest's question, instead she intensified the pace of her steps. They were nearly running when the mount suddenly loomed in front of them. The smell was unbearable for the priest, and he was forced to untangle his hand from Luz's so he could cover his mouth and nostrils.

The hill vaporized. Burning, smoldering garbage heaps were everywhere, and the fouled smoke darkened the atmosphere, cutting down visibility. Father Hugh's eyes began to focus on moving figures enshrouded by the haze. Silhouettes picked their way over the piles, sticking their hands in the refuse, digging, searching.

Suddenly, the priest's attention was caught by something trapped in the soggy ground, and when he looked carefully, the sight that met his eyes made him reel. His breath caught in his throat, and he began to feel dizzy. Among the rotting bones of animals, soiled rags and rusted tin cans, he made out a human leg. Hugh's eyes bulged. His brain swam, and he rubbed his eyes with both hands hoping that the twisted limb would vanish. When he looked again, the leg was still there. He began to tremble, and he turned in the opposite direction with the intention of running away.

"Just a minute, Kid! Not so fast! It's not over yet. We have to face, up front, more of the grief."

The voice knocked the priest off his feet, and the filth that smeared his rump, arms and hands made him gag. Hugh began to cry. Mucus and tears were coursing down his cheeks and chin, and when he wiped his face, he spread the slime on his nose and lips. He retched convulsively.

He moved blindly, without direction. After a few moments of dazed staggering, he turned upward and he saw that Luz was staring intently at a shapeless heap. The priest shakily approached, coming nearer to her. His chest heaved with stress and nausea. His eyes were blurred, and he had to blink several times before his eyes fixed on what it was that the woman was looking at. He shivered as he fell to his knees because his legs were no longer able to support his body. The naked, castrated body of a man lay sprawled on a heap of smoldering garbage, and even though vultures had ripped at parts of his face, Hugh recognized the corpse. It was the man he had seen taken from the High Command.

Luz slowly dropped to her knees, contemplating the remains of the person in front of her. Slowly she rolled over on her haunches, and pulled the body onto her lap. She caressed the mutilated face with her hands, kissing the bloodied cheeks and forehead as she swayed back and forth, moaning softly. Still on his knees, Father Hugh gawked.

Then it began. At first, Father Hugh thought he was hearing it in the remote distance, like the humming of a human being or the soft purring of a machine. The sound grew, taking on shaper tones, becoming harsher as it lost its softness. It grew until it became a guttural howling. Horrified, Hugh realized it was coming from the mountain of slime where Luz now wailed, her mouth agape, her face distorted with pain. Her lament expressed all the anguish she had suffered during her years of futile search. It echoed her disbelief and despair at finding her son only to lose him again on the spot. It was more than her body and soul could bear.

The moaning unnerved the priest and he tried to comfort Luz but she would not stop screaming. Terrified, Hugh pressed his hands against his ears, but as he blocked out the woman's screeching, Augie's voice returned.

"Hugh, is crying?"

He tried not to answer, but he heard his voice stammering in response.

"Eve!"

"Why is she sobbing?"

"Because her son murdered his brother!"

"Why? Why would anybody kill his brother?"

The priest refused to answer; and instead, he wrapped his arms around his head hoping to erase the accusation from his mind.

"Are you sorry, Hugh?"

Luz's crying intensified, but still, he did not answer the question. He clamped shut his eyes hoping to escape, but Augie's voice was relentless. It pressured and reproached him with more questions. Then, as if mesmerized by the litany, Hugh snapped open his eyes, rolling them to the right and to the left, as he concentrated, and listened.

"Hugh, who is sobbing?"

The priest answered. His voice quivered, it was almost a whisper.

"It is the cry of Rachel of Ramah."

"Why is she crying, Hugh?"

"Because her children were slaughtered!"

"Who would slaughter children?"

Hugh clenched his teeth, rejecting the question.

"Hugh, are you sorry?"

Hugh kept quiet. Luz's weeping became louder, more disconsolate, and the voice in Father Hugh's head rose above the wailing.

"Hugh, who is weeping?"

"Mary of Bethlehem."

"No! It is Luz Delcano that you hear! It is her pain that's tearing at your guts. Her grief, and that of thousands of others just like her, is now your hurt. Mine too. I want to know, Hugh. Why is she weeping?"

"Because her son was sacrificed!"

"Sacrificed? What do you mean? I don't understand...!"

"For the love of Christ! Shut up!"

By now Hugh was screeching in hysteria.

"Are you sorry, Hugh?"

The priest cursed, refusing to answer for the third time. Instead, he sprang to his feet, running until he thought his chest would burst. He feared he would choke on the saliva trapped in his throat. He ran down the rotting slopes of El Playón, onto the streets of San Salvador, turning corners, bumping and smashing into walls and people. He lost his way several times, retracing his steps, until he found the direction that took him back to Colonel Delcano.

V

Hugh Joyce made his way to the fortress that housed Colonel Delcano's office. Disregarding the hour, he plunged deep into its inner section where he was halted by guards before he neared the door of the colonel's office. When he was stopped, Hugh began to shout in an effort to get the colonel's attention. The orderly rushed into the office, returning in seconds.

"*Coronel* Delcano will see you now, Señor Joyce."

Hugh entered the room breathing heavily, trying to regain a measure of confidence and composure. He had forgotten that he was encrusted with slime, and that his hair and face were stiff with filth. Colonel Delcano was waiting for him. He gestured toward a chair, indicating to the priest that he sit. He showed his distaste for Hugh's dirty condition by fluttering his nostrils slightly and by tightening his thin lips.

"Father Joyce, it's indeed good to see you once again. I apologize for the disruption that's taking place in our city."

Hugh, not yet in full control of himself, was jarred even more by the title which Delcano had used. He had always been careful to pass as a civilian, as a business associate of Sinclaire Enterprises. The colonel noticed Hugh's confusion, and he smiled thinly.

"So you're surprised. Come now, Father, you really didn't think that you could keep your little secret from me, did you? I've known all along that you're a priest."

Hugh was struggling to keep his balance. Lucio Delcano's pale gaze, however, was unnerving him. The icicles in his voice rubbed the priest's insides, and he was afraid that he would begin to tremble visibly.

"I know a lot more about you, my friend. Much more, believe me. May I humbly admit that I know everything about you and your associate, Mr. Sinclaire, beginning with the day you were born."

Father Hugh thought the floor beneath him was quaking. Again, he wanted to run. The strain of passing the night in the shelter, the traps his mind had been fabricating, along with the horrors of El Playón were taking their toll on him. He knew that his strength was gone, and that he was cracking under the strain of those frozen blue eyes.

"Look, Colonel, I've been under considerable stress and..."

He was cut off by the colonel's upheld hand. It was very white, its fingers long and tapered.

"I understand, my friend. Such violence, so much death. It should not be happening, I admit. Allow me to ask you what I can do for you at this time."

The colonel was speaking in flawless English. His words were pronounced perfectly, and his voice was cool and biting, like a newly sharpened blade.

"I need to return home. I believe you can help me."

"So soon? But you've only been here since...let me see...a little over twenty-four hours."

Colonel Delcano referred to a file on his desk. Father Hugh realized that he had been under the colonel's surveillance since he had first arrived in San Salvador.

"Yes, Sir. I need to report back to my university...that is...I... well...to be frank with you, this whole thing has been a mistake. I didn't realize the extent of the conflict."

"Of course. I understand." The blue gaze was accentuated by an ironic smile. "I'll see to it that you're taken to the airport immediately. There are a few special flights still being allowed. You'll be my guest on one of them. However..."

He again lifted his hand as Hugh was beginning to stand, motioning the priest back to his seat. "However, Father Joyce, there is a matter of importance about which I must speak to you before you leave."

The priest wrinkled his forehead. He wanted to leave, to escape; he had no taste for any more business. Colonel Delcano paused as he peered at the unshaven, dirty face of his former associate.

"There's the matter of the confidentiality of our past business. What was confidential to our association must continue in the same manner. Do you understand me, Father Joyce?"

Colonel Delcano's meaning was clear to Hugh. The implication was that Hugh would in some way disclose their business once he returned to the United States.

"Colonel, I understand you, and you can be sure that I would never, I repeat, never, say or do anything that would jeopardize our transactions. You have my word on it, Sir."

Delcano's hands formed a triangle under his chin, and the muscles of his face were still. His gaze was serene and transparent. He detested Hugh Joyce. Not only was the priest a witness, someone who knew a great deal about the inner workings of the system, but the man was obviously an opportunist and, more than likely, a coward. The colonel knew that Joyce was someone who would bend, or even break, under the pressure of opposition. He had no doubt that the priest now seated in front of him would disclose any information about his dealings in El Salvador if it meant saving his own skin. To further complicate matters, the priest had lost his nerve. It was obvious that even now he was on the brink of a nervous collapse.

Much was at stake, and Colonel Delcano had the obligation to think of his country's welfare. There were several American senators and congressmen, the colonel was convinced, who would gladly move to alter their government's dealings with the High Command, if only they could be provided with the necessary evidence. Hugh Joyce could provide such evidence.

Colonel Delcano sighed wearily. His decision had been made. For a moment, however, his eyes flickered as he turned his gaze on a sheet of paper placed on his desk. He was looking at a report regarding several priests who had died that morning during the street fighting.

"A pity, my friend, that all priests are not as...how should I express it...not as wise as you are."

"I don't understand, Colonel."

"I mean that most of your fellow priests do not share your views on...how to put it...on business transactions in this world of ours. Am I not right?"

"Yes. You are correct. We're not all the same."

Hugh was shivering. Just as he had desired to find the safety of the colonel's office, he now wanted to get out. Delcano sensed the priest's anxiety, and he deliberately allowed minutes to drag by. Both men were silent while the colonel stared at Hugh who sat with his head hanging low over his chest, picking at dirt caught under his fingernails. Colonel Delcano finally shifted in his chair, and turning to the telephone, he ordered a car to come to the front entrance.

Hugh was relieved to see that the interview had ended, and the two men waited in silence for the knock on the door that would signal when the car was ready. Then, when it arrived, the colonel extended his right hand, shaking hands with the priest.

"Good-bye, my friend. I've enjoyed doing business with you. Have a safe journey."

The priest turned, quickly walking out the door and down the stairs, impatient to get away. Soon he would be home, and this nightmare would be behind him.

Just as Hugh was about to enter the car, two soldiers intercepted him with the order to hand over his passport. Hugh was irritated at this unexpected loss of precious time. He tried to explain that he was a personal guest of Colonel Delcano but the soldiers seemed indifferent to whatever Father Hugh said. Instead, they shoved him against a wall and ordered him to empty his pockets of whatever objects he might be carrying. Frustrated and refusing to listen to them, he attempted to get into the waiting car. As he moved, arms outstretched toward the vehicle, a detonation rang out and a bullet pierced his neck, swerving upward to lodge itself in his brain.

From the heights of his window facing the street, the colonel watched the incident unfolding on the street beneath him. He saw the priest's body plummet headlong towards the ground, rebounding as it hit the pavement. He watched the crumpled body convulse momentarily, its fingers twitching and contorting.

The colonel lingered for a few minutes at the window, gazing absentmindedly at the priest's body. He then turned away from the window and approached his desk to re-read the report that had been submitted to him a few minutes before his interview with Hugh Joyce. The report communicated that Luz Delcano had been observed unearthing the body of the executed guerrilla, Bernabé. The wording of the message ended abruptly, conveying no further details of her reaction, nor of her whereabouts.

Colonel Delcano felt his usual impatience with inefficiency, but he let it pass. He called for his aide. When the soldier walked in, Colonel Delcano spoke rapidly.

"Is the lieutenant still on the premises?"

"Sí, Señor. He's waiting for further instructions from you."

"Ask him to come in."

Within a few minutes, the lieutenant appeared, extreme fatigue mirrored on his face. The pupils of his eyes were dilated.

"You've done well today, Teniente. You've followed orders perfectly."

"¡Gracias, mi Coronel!"

"One more thing. Deliver this order to the sergeant presently on duty. He's to implement it this evening."

Delcano handed the lieutenant a sealed envelope. The order was the last one that he would be receiving. It directed his own execution.

The soldier left the office, quietly closing the door behind him. Lucio Delcano sat rigidly at his desk, remaining in that posture for several hours as he thought about his mother and his brother. A numbness was invading his body, paralyzing his heart, and he felt afraid and lost, as he often had when he was a child. His obsession had been fulfilled. His brother was dead, yet Delcano felt empty and sick. Like everything else in his life, even the anticipated elation of vengeance had been denied him.

EPILOGUE

Civil War Ends in El Salvador With Signing of Treaty.

San Salvador—With ringing church bells and exploding fireworks...thousands of Farabundo Martí National Liberation Front guerrillas and their supporters celebrated the end of a 12-year civil war...Francisca Merina looked over the packed plaza with wide eyes. "I came to show my support for so much hope. The armed forces recruited my son eight years ago. They wouldn't give him back to me...later they brought him to me dead."

The Los Angeles Times, January 17, 1992

I

After the guerrilla offensive of November, 1989, the war between the FMLN and government forces continued to ravage El Salvador until the Peace Accord was signed in January, 1992. During the intervening years, disappearances of people continued to afflict countless families. Young men died at the hands of death squads. Scores of Salvadorans fled the city and headed for the countryside hoping to distance themselves from shootings and kidnappings. The flow of refugees escaping the country did not let up.

Luz Delcano survived the violence as well as the grief of losing her son. She was among those people who chose to leave the city where she had witnessed so much death and loss. When the search for her son ended on the slopes of El Playón, two campesinos had helped her carry Bernabé's body from the mount to a secluded place. There, she and the strangers scratched out a hole deep enough to bury his body. They offered to stay with her, but she refused their kindness. Instead, she walked to the fringe of the city where she joined other men and women in the exodus away from the strife.

Luz now lives in the mountains of Chalatenango in a village known as Guarjila.